MW00777531

Copyright © 2023 Keira Montclair

All rights reserved under International and
Pan-American Copyright Conventions

By payment of required fees, you have been granted the
*non*-exclusive, *non*-transferable right to access and read the
text of this book. No part of this text may be reproduced,
transmitted, downloaded, decompiled, reverse engineered,
or stored in or introduced into any information storage
and retrieval system, in any form or by any means, whether
electronic or mechanical, now known or hereinafter
invented without the express written permission of
copyright owner.

**Please Note**

The reverse engineering, uploading, and/or distributing
of this book via the internet or via any other means
without the permission of the copyright owner is illegal
and punishable by law. Please purchase only authorized
electronic editions, and do not participate in or encourage
electronic piracy of copyrighted materials. Your support of
the author's rights is appreciated.

No part of this book may be reproduced or transmitted
in any form or by any electronic or mechanical means,
including photocopying, recording or by any information
storage and retrieval system, without the written permission
of the publisher, except where permitted by law.

Cover Design and Interior format by The Killion Group
thekilliongroupinc.com

# The Scot's Traitor

HIGHLAND HUNTERS 2

# Keira Montclair

# CHAPTER ONE

*Summer, 1315, Edinburgh, Scotland*

"THERE YE ARE, ye vile bastard. I'll put an arrow through yer black heart someday."

Reyna Matheson, daughter of Clan Matheson's chieftain, peered through the leaves of the tree she was perched in to watch the English garrison as it made its way to Berwick Castle, presently controlled by the English bastards. On patrol for the Ramsay group working for King Robert while he was in Ireland, it was their job to be aware of the movements of the English garrison, especially the one led by the cruel Captain Wulfstan de Gray.

The man not far from her perch.

The man who tortured his prisoners with odd tools, had a special chamber built with drains for bodily fluids, and was the most feared man in the English forces.

How she hated the English dogs. She'd never met de Gray, but if she did, she'd do her best to kill the bastard for kidnapping and scaring the hell out of her cousin and best friend, Isla Matheson. How she wished she'd been given clearance to shoot him now. Her bow was her favored weapon, and she was nearly close enough to make a hit.

Dyna and Maitland, the leaders of her patrol, said there was to be no killing at present unless forced to defend yourself.

So she and her cousin, Ysenda Ramsay, remained perched in the tree, watching over the English soldiers. They noted all the comings and goings of the castle, and would report back to Maitland Menzie, the man in charge of her group.

"I count six score," Ysenda whispered. "Ye see the same?"

"Aye," she said, a grin bubbling up before she could control it. "Just a moment. I have to move this branch first or 'twill surely rip my legging." All the women trained by Gwyneth Ramsay, her grandmother, wore leggings and a tunic when in battle. Her grandmother considered skirts foolish, and Reyna had to agree with her. Ysenda's mother, Merewen, made the prettiest ones of all and she would not tear this pair gifted her by Aunt Merewen.

"I saw that, Reyna. What did ye see?" Her cousin was adept at reading clues from Reyna's expressions. She always had been unlike her best friend Isla.

Reyna and Isla had much in common. But while Isla hid her feelings, Reyna did not.

"Naught. Once they are out of sight, we can return to camp." Reyna wouldn't admit to her cousin that she'd seen the one she'd been searching for—the English captain known as The Wolf.

She'd rarely been off Black Isle but she knew all the Clan Matheson people along with most in Clan Ramsay, her mother's clan. Loyal and steadfast to the Scots, she still had a keen curiosity about the strangers in front of her. While the English were their sworn enemies, she couldn't help but be intrigued by the soldiers. She happened to love men, though her sire didn't appreciate her current interests. She had to keep that part of her hidden, but now that she was on her own on a mission, her curiosity was flying high.

Who better to check out the man with the reputation of being the cruelest leader in all of England than the woman who was adept at judging men's characters? He was directly in front of her as the cavalcade passed by. His long dark hair, tethered below the collar of the fine doublet he wore, was distinctive. She'd hoped to see his face. Would he look cruel? Did he have a constant sneer?

Her primary goal was to kill the man. The Wolf had captured Reyna's best friend Isla and Isla's betrothed, Grif, who had also been beaten and tortured. Reyna vowed to see the Wolf pay for his transgressions. It would be sheer pleasure to put an arrow right between his eyes. But not before she got a good look at the man. She wished to ask him what would make a man so cruel.

Her interest in behavior was more than piqued. Had he been tortured as a child? Did the Scots capture him so he was interested in revenge? Aunt Jennet, who considered herself an expert on men's behavior, would say he was born that way. But was he? What emotion drove such cruelty? She'd probably never know because if given the chance, she'd kill the man for the assault on her clanmates.

Isla and Grif were back on Ramsay land, where they could heal from their captivity. They would return and meet them in Berwick, she'd been told. She couldn't wait to see how Isla fared.

Wulf strode along as if he were more important than anyone on God's green meadows. Men were such a mystery to her.

She continued to watch him, seek out all she could about the man, but then she made a critical mistake.

She dropped her bow.

It wouldn't have been an issue, but the Wolf heard, stopping his horse and turning it around to stare directly at her.

"Uh-oh," Ysenda whispered.

A ripple of excitement traveled up Reyna's spine. There was naught she loved more than the thrill of exhilaration from confrontation in battle; she didn't have much experience outside of training and small border skirmishes, but she loved the energy and excitement that coursed through her body during a fight.

She whispered, "Dinnae move, Ysenda. Ye know he cannae see us through the leaves."

Reyna chewed on her lower lip, hoping she was correct. There were only two archers against a garrison of Englishmen. A daunting ratio, even for two trained Ramsay archers. But as he grew nearer to their spot in the trees, she felt herself leaning to get a closer look at him. She knew now was not the right time to confront the man, but she was drawn to him in a way that was even greater than her desire to murder him for what he'd done to Isla and Grif. It made no sense to her, but she found herself wondering if the man thought her beautiful or homely. The anticipation gave her a tingle in her nether region.

She knew exactly when the Wolf caught sight of her. He guided his brown stallion directly toward their tree at a raging gallop that frightened Reyna.

"Drop down!" she yelled to Ysenda as she herself climbed down, retrieving her fallen bow before mounting the horse she had hidden behind the bushes.

Ysenda was already ahead of her, mounting her white mare and shooting back down the path away from the castle.

"Bloody bastard," Reyna squealed.

She tugged on the reins and sent her horse into a full gallop, taking him down the path a ways, casting quick glances back over her shoulder to see where the Englishman was and if he was alone.

Alone and gaining on her. "Ysenda, go straight to Maitland. I'm drawing him the other route."

Ysenda nodded and set off, now way ahead of Reyna, her golden plait bouncing against her shoulders. Reyna turned to the forest, intending to take the Englishman through the overgrown paths that she knew so well. She loved riding more than anything.

"Goldie," she whispered to her beloved chestnut horse. "We can beat him. No Englishman can ride a horse like a Scotswoman. We'll show him."

She led the man down a separate path into the forest, leaping over logs and small burns through an area where she had to duck to keep the branches from ripping the tender skin on her cheeks. Goldie crashed through the brush as though she were the greatest buck with a head full of antlers. Reyna's insides bubbled and churned with the excitement of the chase, the ride, and the lovely day all spurring her forward. The heat of the chase and the potential capture sent her pulse into a rapid beat that she loved.

He drew closer.

And closer.

Close enough that Reyna's jaw tensed, wondering what the hell would happen if she were captured. Would he ravish her on the fine moss of the forest? Or chain her to his horse and drag her across the meadow they'd just left? He could try, but he'd not succeed at either one, because she would take him by surprise with her dagger. No one expected a lass to be trained with a dagger like she was. Her grandmother had insisted they all had that skill—lads and lasses.

Reyna relished the feel of the cool hilt in the palm of her hand.

She had an odd feeling course through her body, surely more pleasant than she should have at this point. But another look back eliminated that feeling by changing it to fear.

Now he was too close.

He could take her for a spy and attempt to hang her.

Reyna pushed her horse faster, racing through the woods, her mount thundering through the brush. Her heart raced with the thrill of escape, but her throat went dry with the awareness that his mount would wear her horse down in no time.

But then he disappeared.

The man took a different path, a mistake on his part. He'd probably thought to cut her off, but he struggled to keep up.

Glancing back at her valiant pursuer one more time, she barked out a laugh when his horse missed the last jump over a fallen tree, sending its master flying through the air and landing with a bellow. She checked back one more time to make sure the man got up, and he did. A scorching shout and a fist toward her told her the Wolf was just fine.

She waved to him over her shoulder and continued on to their well-hidden camp, confident that he'd never catch her now.

That had been as entertaining as anything she'd done since their mission to watch over the Borderlands while King Robert the Bruce traveled to Ireland to assist his brother. She knew Ysenda would yell at her because she took too many chances, but she couldn't seem to stop herself.

After all that had happened to her best friend, Reyna's life had become a mass of confusion and uncertainty. Isla had always been by her side. They'd left Black Isle together, but Isla was on Ramsay land now instead of continuing the patrol.

Of all the galling behaviors Isla could have committed, getting betrothed and handfasting before Reyna was not one she expected. The two were born on the same day over twenty years ago and had been inseparable since then. But there was one main characteristic difference between the two of them.

Isla didn't like men. Reyna loved them.

So no matter how she tried to imagine why her dear friend had handfasted, she couldn't come up with a suitable reason. Ysenda had said it was because Isla and her beloved Grif had been held as prisoners together—twice. And Dyna had agreed with Ysenda, explaining that forced time together changed the way anyone would feel about the partner they'd been confined with. Going through such a traumatic event, held by the English, possibly tortured, had given the two something they shared that no one else could claim.

And so they'd handfasted.

The two had gone to Ramsay land, Isla seeking her grandparents' approval, and were to return to the mission soon, but she hadn't seen either one yet. It was probably a blessing because she still had no idea how to greet her best friend. No matter how Reyna looked at it, her best friend had a new partner in her life.

And it wasn't Reyna.

She came through the trees to find Ysenda waiting for her. "I thought you'd finally done it, Reyna." She let out a huge sigh of relief, smiled, then led the way back to their camp. "How long did he follow ye?"

Reyna gave her the answer that was most appropriate. "Until his horse missed a jump and tossed him on his arse."

She didn't answer honestly. Reyna's thoughts were only one thing.

The Wolf hadn't followed her long enough to satisfy her curiosity. Of that much, she was certain. There had to be much more to this mysterious villain. She wished to know everything about the man before she plunged her dagger into his black heart.

# CHAPTER TWO

WULFSTAN DE GRAY cursed at the beautiful lass who'd led him on a harsh chase, her comely arse bouncing on her saddle in such a way he had visions of her bobbing that fine bottom on his lap.

Both of them unclothed.

That would never happen. Though the lass intrigued him, his mission in this border town had nothing to do with seducing young women. And all he had to do was remember his own vulnerable sister to remind him that he'd never act dishonorably to a young woman. Not even one who perched in a tree to spy on him. He laughed ruefully at the irony. But then again, how many times had they encountered a female in battle?

He snorted at that thought because the answer came so quickly. Never.

He climbed on his horse and headed back to his garrison, catching up as they arrived at Berwick Castle. As he approached the gates, he heard Emmot calling out to him, "Where the hell is she, Captain? You didn't catch up with her?"

Emmot was his second in command and the man he trusted most in the world. Finding Emmot in the crowd, Wulf could see the man had a twinkle in his eye that he would like to beat out of him. He pulled his horse abreast of Emmott's and shrugged before speaking quietly to his friend.

"You know the Scots have better mounts than we do, and the one she had, was one of the finest. That horse could run an obstacle course like the strongest stallion, probably better because being a mare, she had more grace, and her rider weighs less. Why the hell our king cannot get us mounts like that is a question that forever bothers me."

Emmot snorted. "I think I know something else that will forever bother you now, a fine arse bouncing on that horse."

Wulf cast an acknowledging glare at Emmot at the same time he reached down to rearrange himself. He wasn't about to let himself build an erection like he had when he'd been chasing the woman. It had been too painful when he'd taken the fall. "I wish to know which clan those women are from. They wear breeches like a man." Better than any man, in his opinion.

They crossed under the portcullis into Berwick Castle, surrounded by a score of his men, so he set the question to the group. "That lass. What clan trains female archers and allows them to wear men's clothing like the ones in Carlisle? She was from the same clan. Does anyone know?"

"I do, Captain." A young man behind him answered meekly.

"Speak up, man. What clan of the Scots are they from?"

"Mostly Ramsays. Gwyneth Ramsay was a spy working under King Alexander before he died. She was the best archer in all the land. She trains her daughters and granddaughters. Even sews their clothing, those fine breeches that stick to their legs like skin." The group dismounted as the stable lads raced over to care for their mounts.

Another soldier he didn't know well chimed in, "She makes those leggings so they cling to their sweet arses, just like I'd like to…" Wulf's hand swung out hard and slapped his cheek, enough to surprise each of the men around him, though they all kept their tongue.

"Never speak of women like that. Think as you wish, but never say it. Would you speak of your own mother as such? Disrespect your own sister? Five lashes to the next man who speaks as such in front of me."

He stormed off toward the castle, Emmot hurrying to keep up with him.

He knew that slap would add to the rumors about him—how cruel he was, how he tortured his prisoners. Any number of false rumors always followed the true tales. He'd never let on the truth because having his men fear him as much as the enemy was better. But there was also some truth to any rumor. The truth?

That he was a heartless bastard. True, because he had good reason to hate nearly everyone.

That he would strike without warning. He'd just proven that rumor to be true.

The rest he ignored. There was no sense in listening to falsehoods all day. He would gain nothing from it. His mission was to lead the English garrison as instructed, and as soon as the opportunity arose, he would save his sister from their sire.

Emmot asked, "Any orders for the men? I'll pass them on."

"Go to the kitchens and order their dinner. It is nearly dark. Meat pies and a mug of mead each before they find their bed in the stables or the grass around it. Too many to sleep in the hall, and it bodes to be a fine night. I'll decide where we go next on the morrow."

"Aye, Captain."

He'd never be able to explain to a group of men like this garrison why he was so sensitive to the insults to women, but he loved his mother when she'd been alive, and he still adored his sister.

They were the only two people in his life who had been worth loving.

His father was a bastard.

---

That night, the lasses sat around in their makeshift camp outside Berwick Castle, well-hidden in the woods. Reyna and Ysenda would sleep under a fine tent the Matheson men had crafted for Reyna and Isla. It fit almost all the lasses, but Dyna preferred to sleep under the stars.

Reyna, Ysenda, and Ceit sat around the fire, all sitting on logs and munching on bread that Lewis had brought back from their quick trip to

Ramsay land. Isla and Grif hadn't returned yet, instead going on to Black Isle.

Reyna sighed. "I still cannae believe Isla and Grif are handfasted."

"They may not be. Maitland said they had told everyone about their relationship, but they said betrothed," Ysenda reminded her. "He didn't know if they would marry on Ramsay land, but he didn't think so since her family is on Black Isle. Maitland said they would return once Grif had healed from his beating in the jail."

Ceit said, "I cannae believe his uncle Ellar paid that lass to accuse him of assaulting her. Can you imagine being tossed in jail for something you didn't do? Ellar is daft, for sure. And how did he find a lass willing to accuse Grif of attacking her? If he hadn't been with us, she could possibly have made them all believe it was true. What is wrong with a lass like that? I'll never understand why she did it."

"For coin. 'Tis a simple thing," Ysenda said. "You can get nearly anything done if you pay enough."

"'Tis still a horrific trick to accuse a man of something he didnae do," Ceit muttered.

"Either way, Grif is free, so we dinnae need to worry about him anymore. Grif and Isla will be happy together. I truly believe it." Ysenda reached into a big kettle for a cooked rabbit bone to gnaw on.

"But why Isla? I dinnae understand it. I thought for sure I would meet someone first," Reyna complained, her cheek resting in the palm of her hand. "Everyone said I would be the first to marry. You know they've given me names about my beauty over the years. People on Black Isle like to wager who I'll marry, but I dinnae like to brag."

"But yet ye are," Ysenda drawled, arching a brow at her.

"My apologies, but I cannae right this in my head."

Ceit asked, "Did ye truly think ye would be first? Why would ye think so? Ye are both the same age, born on the same day. Ye could fall in love in another moon, ye never know. Look how fast it happened to Isla. I think ye shouldnae concern yerself. What does it matter who is first?" She brushed the crumbs from her lap and then stared at Reyna, waiting for her answer. Ceit, daughter of Sorcha and Cailean MacAdam, was a beauty in her own right, looking very much like her mother.

"I suppose it doesnae, but being the same age, we've always been a wee bit competitive. Of course, it carried over into our romantic lives. I've kissed more than Isla, so I should marry first." Reyna rubbed both sides of her head at the same time. "Why? She never liked men like I do. Why? I feel like such a failure."

"Ye are making too much of this, and I dinnae understand why," Ysenda said. "Besides, they are handfasted. If ye find a nice Scottish captain, ye could still marry before she does."

Dyna, the female leader of their group, approached the lasses, grabbed a piece of the bread loaf, then stopped. "My guess is that finding a man was Reyna's reason for coming. Even better, to find a husband. I was like Isla, never interested. But then along came Derric, and we were married in no time. 'Tis no surprise to me that she married quickly. She's not the kind of person to mull over something. Ye are, Reyna. And a wee bit spoiled too."

"I am no' spoiled," Reyna declared, nearly slapping her thigh with her hand but realizing how it would look just in time. "I hate it when people say that. Why does everyone say that?" She glanced from Dyna's face to Ysenda and Ceit, hoping for an explanation. She really wished to know so she could prove them wrong. "No one ever calls my brothers spoiled, and we have the same parents."

Ceit said, "Because Hawk and Merek arenae spoiled at all. Yer father wouldnae allow it, but ye are his wee princess. Ye and Kara."

Dyna flopped down onto a tree stump. "Reyna, 'tis because ye have everything ye could ever want. I dinnae believe anyone who says that thinks on yer personality, but of your possessions."

"Please explain. What possessions?" Flabbergasted at the explanation, she had to force herself to continue to listen without arguing.

Ysenda pointed to the tent. "Who made that for ye? Because I'm also a Ramsay, and I dinnae have a fine tent like that. My father is your uncle, yet I have never seen a tent that fine ever."

"My sire made it for me. I see no surprise in that. So he worries about me. No reason to call me spoiled." She scowled at the implication. "Ye wouldnae refuse it either."

Dyna added, "And yer clothing. How many gowns and how many sets of leggings have ye?"

"I have many, but I make most of them. And Grandmama makes some of them. She made the ones I'm wearing, and she's grandmother to Ceit and Ysenda, so theirs are the same." She pulled on the soft forest green fabric of her tightly woven breeches. Was it her mother who insisted on having the finest fabric or her grandmother? She honestly didn't know.

Ceit tugged on the coarse wool of her leggings. "Not here."

Ysenda giggled when she pulled on her own. "None here either."

"I will speak to Aunt Sorcha and Aunt Merewen the next time I see them. They need to buy finer material." It wasn't her fault that her mother was so fussy.

Dyna said, "The softest ever, yet keeps ye warm. Where does she find that material? Brigid must go to Inverness for it."

Reyna shrugged because she had no idea where her mother found the fabric. The shrug earned a snort from Dyna. "Clothing and a tent. Not enough to be spoiled."

Ceit pointed to Reyna's horse, Goldie. "Ye have the best horse after Dyna."

"Again, 'twas a gift from yer sire, Dyna. Grandsire insisted I ride a horse who was a descendant of Midnight. And Ysenda, yer horse is also a descendant of Midnight."

Dyna grinned. "I cannae fault ye for that. I love my horse too." Her grandfather Alex had ridden the best horse in the Battle of Largs. The nearly-black horse known as Midnight was legendary. "Dinnae worry about it. Forget the comments because they arenae true. But ye still need to fix yer mind. It doesnae matter who marries first. Are ye that desperate for a husband?"

Reyna explained the way she felt the best she could. "I'm the chieftain's daughter, so I am always watched. I've heard of men who won't approach me because of who I am. I always hear them whispering about Marcas this and Marcas that. Once that conversation ends, the men go in the opposite direction. Ye'd think I had some terrible sickness. This is my first chance to be far away from Black Isle and Ramsay land. The first time I willnae feel like I'm always being watched. Freedom from an overprotective mother and father."

"I understand that feeling exactly," Ysenda said. Her father, Gavin, had often acted the same.

Ceit added, "Aye, the same for me. All I ever hear is how MacAdam would kill them if they touched me. Cailean MacAdam has such a bad reputation that sometimes I wish he wasnae my sire." She gave a wee pout, and Reyna understood.

Dyna stood and said, "I would suggest ye get yer mind away from finding a man or ye'll end up kidnapped too. Ye have to stay focused. Looking for romance will make ye soft when ye are in battle. Besides, if ye forget it, 'tis more likely to happen."

Dyna froze, and Reyna jumped up.

"What is it? Dyna? Are ye hale?"

The look on their leader's face frightened her. Dyna was known as a seer, but only for people she knew well, not strangers. Her skills did not work on the English garrison.

When her gaze changed, she glanced over at Reyna and whispered, "Ye will be married before the end of the year."

"I will?" She grinned but then scowled. "Who?"

"'Tis a Scotsman, but I cannae tell because I dinnae know him, but he will come to ye."

Reyna relaxed. "That pleases me. Then I can focus on my other goal." She flung the rabbit bones into the forest and sat down again.

"Which is?" Ysenda asked.

"I'm going to kill Wulfstan de Gray." She didn't add what she'd thought all along. If she could kill the English garrison's most dreaded leader, then every Scot would wish to meet her.

There was always planning behind any of Reyna's ideas.

Killing the most dreaded English captain will make every Scot know her name.

Then they'll wish to meet her, and she can choose her own husband.

She'd be damned if she'd let the man choose her. Reyna was always in control.

Now if she could only find a man who would take a step back.

# CHAPTER THREE

A MISSIVE CAME THE next morning, and he was pleased. The messenger from King Edward was clear. The garrison was to stay and protect Berwick Castle. After the recent attack on Carlisle Castle by the Scots, the king favored protecting Berwick Castle. His group only had to keep a faction of knights and soldiers inside the castle at all times while the rest of the garrison patrolled the area to make sure there were no other bands making camp.

He wasn't worried about any small groups, only the large ones. After all, his men stood at over one hundred, so any cluster under a score wasn't worth his time.

Neither were two lasses in breeches, though he wished he could search for the one who rode her horse like any queen of England would. She was definitely a fine beauty, but he didn't have room for that in his life at the moment. All he needed to do was keep the area in Berwick quiet, keep any marauders at bay, so he could focus on what he needed to focus on—finding his sire.

Wulf didn't have time to waste thinking about

romantic interludes. He hadn't had many women in his life, but he'd had enough to learn the fine appreciation of the female anatomy. Still, he couldn't allow even this fine Scottish lass to distract him from his responsibilities.

Emmot said, "Where would you like to patrol, Captain de Gray?"

It was the middle of the day when the sun was highest, a perfect time to patrol. "South of the castle, into the woods where the camps would be found. We'll take ten men, and Henry can take the other ten to go west."

Henry sat awaiting his orders and motioned for his men to take their leave. Once the group split up, Wulf pointed down the path they were to take.

Once they hit a fork in the road, he sent Emmot down one path while he took the other. "Take the men with you. I believe this goes nowhere, so I'll catch up to the rear of the group soon. If we get separated, I'll meet you in the burgh."

He headed down the path, not surprised to find it empty and overgrown. There was an old hut at the end, appearing unused and uninhabited by any person, though he would bet there would be a few creatures inside. Turning his horse around, he froze when he heard the lilt of female giggles. He moved toward the sound, in through the brush, surprised to find an open meadow and one woman riding her horse, clearly enjoying every minute of the outing.

It was the same woman he'd chased before. He stayed in the shadows of the lush summer leaves, hoping he could watch for a short bit. She hadn't seen him yet.

Wulf couldn't have gone after her if he tried, his constitution frozen by the lovely being in front of him, unlike anyone he'd ever seen before. A true vision in her breeches, she mesmerized him simply because watching the grace as she rode as if one with her horse, the beast responding to the smallest movements from the girl's knees, was amazing. Wulf held back a frown as he watched her ride. He'd never seen anything like her, not even in his mother's tales of the goddess Rhiannon. She was a vision to behold, the most beautiful warrior he'd ever seen, and it was more pleasant watching her ride than chasing after her. Would he have to chase her again?

He held his breath as she attempted to stand on the horse, finally managing it for a short while before she fell back onto the horse with a laugh, grabbing the reins and hugging her horse at the same time.

While he enjoyed the short interlude of rider and horse, he also knew she was a Scot, and her continued presence meant she was probably with a group camping close by somewhere. He quietly shifted his weight and cursed silently to himself as he realized he had caught her attention. A moment later, she and her animal flew in the opposite direction.

But he ignored her. Much as he would have loved to capture the lass and keep her to himself, he couldn't do it. He'd enjoyed chasing her before, but he'd made the mistake of thinking his horse was more adept than hers. He'd paid the price by falling from his horse while she laughed gleefully over his failure.

Just once, he'd like to have the lass within a hand's length. He wished to see her up close so he could take in everything about her—the color of her lips, the silkiness of her hair, the hue of her eyes, even her scent. Would it be floral or musky? Would her eyes betray her fear or show fearsomeness?

He had the oddest inkling that she would be one of the most formidable adversaries he would ever encounter, but he couldn't delay his purpose on this day. The lass would have to wait.

This time, it wasn't worth the chance, so he left and headed back into the burgh. He had a meeting with one of England's most notorious men in one of the local inns, a man who he'd counted on over the years to give him sage advice, something he couldn't count on from his own sire. He'd idolized the man and his reputation because he had the unusual ability of never being seen yet knowing everything.

When he arrived at their meeting place, he couldn't stop his mind from wandering, something that had never happened to him. His usual habits were to think on two things only— how to pay his father back for all the wrongdoing he'd done to his children, and how to protect his sister.

Now he found his mind doing strange things. Landing on a certain fiery brunette who could ride a horse like no other. He had the sudden visual image of her in just a chemise on her horse, her waist-length dark hair free and unbound as she stopped in front of him, boldly slipping from her mount and stepping until she stood in front of him, a slight smirk on her lips, her hair covering her breasts so he couldn't see the color of her areolas. Would they prove to be the slightest blush of a peach or a rich dark red of a ripe cherry?

He wrested his attention to the older man who awaited Wulf's arrival, standing impatiently with his arms crossed in front of him.

"Greetings, Wulf. You'll want to know that your father is on the move. He's headed south toward York."

"My sire? Hell, but this is a bad time. I've just brought my garrison to Berwick."

"He'll not be there long, but he'll go deeper into England than Berwick. Tryana is with him."

Wulf couldn't stop himself from staring off into space, scratching his chin, a long held habit that came from trying to keep his hands busy to keep from punching his bastard of a father. Their conversation continued for a bit longer, but his mind always returned to his father.

"Stop worrying about what others think of Wulfstan. Take care of whatever deeds must pass and forget the cruelty. Time to think of other things. Someday it will be time to create a family of little wolves."

"Many thanks for the update. I wish I could stay, but I must move on to see to my men."

"Wait. I have a favor to ask." The man explained

what he wanted him to do, and it seemed a simple task.

"I'd be honored to help you."

The man gave him the details he needed to complete the task so he listened carefully, taking in all the fine points and locking them into his mind. This would prove to be a profitable venture to take on while he tracked his father and sister.

"Godspeed. And do not forget our agreement."

"It is secured in my mind. Godspeed with you." He walked away from their meeting in a trance, visions of the man he hated more than anyone else making him change all his plans. He didn't know how this new assignment would change things, but he'd have to make adjustments. When he knew his father had passed on through, everything else would change.

Stepping out of the building and back into the overcast and misty afternoon, he mounted his horse and rode down the center of Berwick. He scanned the faces as he passed but saw nothing worth further examination.

When he finally headed out of town, he caught sight of the lass as she exited a nearby inn alone. He forced his father out of his mind and focused on the girl whose continued reappearance was beginning to feel like no coincidence. And she was alone. This would be the perfect time to do what he wished to do.

He waited to see which way she headed, ruminating over what he was about to do and making sure it was a good decision he could defend. This was a perfect opportunity to apprehend the lass. It was his duty. Any Scot in Berwick needed to be questioned and he knew it would please his commander, indeed King Edward himself, if Wulf could find out who the head of her group was and where they were at.

It had nothing to do with her beauty, brilliance, or love for life.

Or did it?

She made her way to her horse which had been tied to a bush down the street, mounted with the help of a boulder, and headed out of town. Wulf followed. He had to learn her identity. It was said she was a Ramsay, but he had to know for certain which one she was. Unfortunately, he saw another horsewoman headed toward her, two other horses flanking the woman.

It was his chance now or forget ever searching for her. He spurred his horse forward, moving as fast as he dared, catching up with her at about the same time she turned to face him, but he took her off guard, so he leaned over, snaked his arm around her waist, and yanked her off her horse, landing her in front of him, nearly on his lap.

The two struggled as she did her best to fight him off, attempting to jump, but they were moving too fast. "Stop, or I'll go back and put my sword in your horse's chest."

That stopped her.

Her eyes widened, and she stilled. "Ye wouldnae dare."

"Take your chance and see if I would," he growled, tightening his hold.

After realizing he was serious and really would

kill her horse, she stopped thrashing in his arms, but she said arrogantly, "Let me go, ye brute. I'll happily get off yer lap once I've bashed ye over the head with my fist and impaled ye with my dagger."

He grinned. "That's what I'm counting on." He heard the sound of her drawing her dagger and quickly pressed her face into his chest in an attempt to stop her. "Don't try to use it," he warned, "or I'll take you to the ground, and you won't be getting back up."

She tensed beside him.

"Did you hear me?" he growled.

"Aye." She slowly relaxed against him. "I heard ye."

Damn, but she was so warm and soft in his arms that he didn't want to let her go. "We'll have to discuss this further when I'm not holding you on my lap," he muttered, his arms secure around her.

"We'll do nae such thing," she snapped. "Ye're going to let me go, and I'm going to unsheathe my dagger and cut yer throat."

"We'll see." He chuckled, pleased with her fiery spirit. He shouldn't be because it would make her a much more difficult captive, but it would surely make their time together more interesting while he waited for King Edward to arrive. "Now fix yourself as we have a ways to go."

He helped her maneuver until she faced forward in the saddle in front of him, and she glanced back once in a fury, her forest green eyes matching her tunic perfectly. But he also caught something else in that one glance.

She was the most beautiful woman he'd ever seen.

———∿∿———

Reyna fought to hold on, but then she caught the fury in his gaze. Her abductor had to be the man known as the Wolf of the English army. She would not allow his reputation to intimidate her.

Bouncing uncomfortably on the man's legs and the saddle of the horse, she grabbed onto his arm that had a hold of the reins and leaned over, biting him through the sleeve of his doublet. He bellowed in pain and rage, and she was please to know she'd hurt him.

"Do that again, and I will go back and make you watch while I kill your horse. I know how much that beast means to you." He grabbed her plait and yanked her up, leaving her scrambling to get into a decent position. Finally reseated in front of him, she panted but never said a word, refusing to shed even one tear in front of him.

"Let. Me. Go." Her words came out as a hiss aimed directly at him. How she wished she could be a snake and snap at his neck.

"My, aren't you a feisty one? We could have a very interesting time together. My apologies, dearest, but I'm keeping you."

His smirk made her wish to punch him. "I'm no' a possession. Ye cannae just keep me," she said through gritted teeth, refusing to give in to her fear of what was to come.

"Ah, but in war, I can. We are at war if you have not noticed. Or you would not have been back

at Carlisle Castle with all your group attempting
to put an arrow in my arse. You have a fine aim,
so you'll not have access to a bow anytime soon."

"Where are ye taking me?" That much she
knew from her grandparent's teachings, that it was
her job to find out as much as she could about
where she was going, where she would be kept,
and how to find her way out. True, many who
had been captured in the past were saved by the
Ramsay and Matheson warriors, but some had
to make their own escape. Her mother's words
carried with her. "Ye need to follow where ye go,
look for landmarks, even when inside the castle.
Above or below stairs? In the dungeon? If ye are
captured, 'tis important ye keep yer wits so ye can
help yerself too."

"Should be no surprise to you that we are
headed to Berwick Castle. It's where you've been
spying, isn't it? You and however many there are
of you. You've been sent from Carlisle Castle to
Berwick Castle, watching and waiting to pounce
now that your king has gone to Ireland."

Oh, but how she detested his smugness, that
attitude that said he knew more than anyone.
"Bloody bastard, I dinnae care what ye know of
me, you'll no' keep me. My group will come for
me. And if they dinnae, then my sire will come
for me, bringing a force of Scots that will tear ye
to pieces. He'll start from Black Isle, then stop at
Clan Grant, Clan Cameron, Clan Ramsay, and
more. And if no' my sire, then my grandfather and
grandmama. Ye may know them. The Ramsays?
Logan and Gwyneth, the spies?"

"My apologies, but I do not keep up on the clans of you savage Scots. While I have heard the name before, it was just in passing, nothing important."

"Ye havenae heard of how my grandmama, Gwyneth Ramsay, is the best archer in all of Scotland and has pinned a man to a tree by his bollocks?" That brought a gurgle of laughter from the man, as if it started in his boots and crept up his belly until it bubbled out of his mouth. A gleeful laugh that she hated. She'd be thinking of some way to hurt this man while he held her captive. Any chance she got she would kick, bite, and scratch until he could not wait to be rid of her. Put a dagger within her reach and she'd stab him. "Dinnae believe me. Ye shall regret it someday soon."

He ignored her, instead focusing on the road ahead of them.

As they neared the back of the castle her belly began doing flip-flops because no one had approached them from behind. She had expected Dyna to chase them. She glanced over her shoulder, looking for any of her group, but the path was empty.

"Don't get your hopes up. The rest of my men took care of your small group. You can count on it. If any survived, they will not come for you." He slowed his horse which told her he really was not worried about anyone catching up with him.

Reyna twisted at the waist to get a good look at the man who sat behind her, not surprised that he was as handsome as she'd guessed from afar. He had long dark hair, nearly black, his deep blue eyes looking more like the ice on their loch on a sunny winter day than the warmth of the blue sky. A strong jawline did not budge when he locked his gaze onto hers.

The man held a great deal of pain in those eyes, probably the cause of his cold attitude. His slight bit of stubble made him appear older than he probably was. "How many years have ye?" she asked out of curiosity.

"Five and twenty. And you?"

"Twenty."

"Just a wee babe out fighting for King Robert. He has no conscience forcing women to fight for him."

"I choose to be here." She stopped her sentence as they turned a corner and headed for the portcullis, not surprised to see several of his men awaiting his arrival. They moved their horses back, allowing him to pass through the middle of them. When he'd gone halfway, he stopped his horse, then let his gaze roam over the dozen or so men surrounding him. Once he had all their attention, he announced, "This woman is my captive. If anyone dares to touch her for any reason, you'll get ten lashes. Any questions?"

"Just one," the smallest of them asked. "Who is she?"

"I don't know yet, but I will." He smirked, then moved his horse toward the castle gates, traveling over the moat and under the portcullis, dismounting on the other side. He moved to help her down, but she slapped his hand out of the way and jumped off the horse, landing directly in front of him.

She had to look up at his tall frame, the gray clouds moving swiftly over his head as she assessed him, and he did the same to her, though his eyes gave away nothing. He spun her around and tied her hands behind her back with a fine piece of rope.

He pushed her in front of him, and the crowd of soldiers stepped aside, allowing them to pass. Reyna felt as if she were a piece of meat, each man staring at various parts of her body and deciding what they would do to her if given a chance. She squared her shoulders and kept her eyes away from all of them, focusing instead on the tall, narrow-shouldered warrior who led her just a few steps ahead to the keep inside the curtain wall of Berwick Castle.

Then one man dared to reach for her breast, though he missed.

She jerked away from him. "Gwyneth Ramsay is my grandmother. Have ye no' heard of her?" she called out to the men as she passed them.

"Close your mouth," The Wolf said, stepping to her side.

She smirked because she got exactly the reaction she was looking for. At least half of the soldiers covered their private parts, though some tried to do it discreetly. Her mother had once told her that grandmama's reputation had spread far and wide, and now she believed it. It was Bethia's daughter Thea who had reminded them all of her grandmother's feat. "My mother still talks about

Aunt Gwyneth. She was so furious that the man had dared to bury yer mother and Aunt Jennet in a box that she aimed for his privates."

Everyone knew that Gwyneth Ramsay never missed. Oh, she did these days because her vision had failed a wee bit, but she had the skills of legends.

She couldn't help but taunt the men a wee bit more. "She'll come for me, beware. And I'm a witch." Then she hissed.

The Wolf yanked on her bindings. "What is wrong with you? Have you no idea how a lady acts?"

"A lady stands up for herself and does not cower to a man. 'Tis how I was raised."

"Ignore her ramblings," he said to his men.

But her words had settled on some of them. All had been ready to grab her and fondle her, but they'd dropped their outstretched arms at Wulf's threat. Her words caused some of them to take a step back and turn sideways. A reaction that protected their private area.

Her gaze locked on the castle in front of them. The fortress was built upon a tall hill, with a fortified wall of stone surrounding the top. The sides were steep and dropped into a deep canyon that had been carved through the rock. The landscape outside the castle was breathtakingly beautiful, with sandy beaches and green forest that continued right down to the shore. She could hear the sound of the waves crashing onto the sand, and it took her breath away. She always felt breathless the first time she visited a new place. Her homeland was a small village nestled by the sea on Black Isle, but the peninsula there was a rocky coastline. Now, the sun peeked out between the clouds, showing off the beauty of the surroundings of the castle simply because Berwick Castle sat so high on the coastline. Looking off into the distance, the sea sparkled like a diamond in the sunlight, reflecting back its vibrant blue color.

She reminded herself that as a captive of the English army there would be no enjoying the beach. She was not the first Scot to be taken, nor even the first of her clans to be taken. Isla had survived the dungeon, so she would also.

Glancing over at her captor, she wished to memorize everything there was about this mysterious man known as the Wolf. He was a handsome man, dark brooding eyes hiding whatever atrocities had happened in his past. Or would they be thinking on the atrocities he'd committed as captain of the English garrison? His skin, bronzed by the sun, carried no imperfections, no scars, no wrinkles in the corners of his eyes. If they'd met under different circumstances, if he were a Scottish man of honor, things could be different between them.

But she was his captive, and she had to get away from him before he decided to commit a few of those atrocities on her. Her mother and her aunt Jennet had been taken captive multiple times at much younger ages than she was. Her aunt Jennet's words stayed with her more than her own mother's because she'd admitted to crying and depending on Jennet to save the two of them. But it was Aunt Jennet who'd said, "Never let them know ye are scared. Men dinnae know how to handle strong women. Show them ye are stronger than they are, and ye'll win."

If this man was truly The Wolf, then she needed to be stronger than ever. But she reminded herself that her clan was strong, and they'd soon learn she was taken. Someone would come for her before she was hurt.

Wouldn't they?

# CHAPTER FOUR

WULF LED HER to one of the towers at the far side of the castle, the only place in the keep where she would possibly be safe. He closed his eyes with exasperation as he followed the sweetest arse he'd ever seen up the staircase to the chamber at the top of the tower. It was the only place he knew he could protect the woman from the wandering hands of the men in the castle.

Other than the cook and the kitchen maids, he'd only seen a couple of other housekeeping maids about, so there was little chance the hundred or so men would see their needs met. And she was a mighty pretty dish.

They'd be asking for her.

They'd be searching for her.

Once inside, he said, "You'll be my captive until I decide to let you go. I will not hurt you, but trust me, if you try to talk sweetly to any other men, they will hurt you. Do not trust any of them. They'd love to take what they want and throw you away when they are finished. And I do believe if one man convinced you to trust him, when he finished with you, he would offer you to all the men. They are not used to noble women like you."

He circled the chamber, pacing slowly, while she stood in the middle, her hands folded demurely in front of her.

She was as demure as a female brown bear protecting its cubs. She was also so beautiful he had to force his gaze away from her, fearing his expression would tell her how he truly felt. "If you look around the room where you will be spending the next moon, I'm sure you'll see you have been given better treatment than some of your friends were given in Carlisle. That bed is yours, you have a screen to change behind, and I will bring you a meal twice a day. Only as long as you are agreeable."

He stopped in his pacing and turned to face her.

She twirled gracefully with barely a movement of her boot until she stood directly in front of him. "What do ye want of me?"

His gaze went from the long chestnut brown hair, the splash of freckles across her nose, to the luscious pink lips and down to her neck where the small sensitive bone sat patiently awaiting his lips, and finally to the voluptuous curves below. The way her clothing clung to those curves was sinful in his eyes, though very few women could wear them the way this woman did. "Not much. I will keep you until the enemy is gone. I wish for your friends to go back to the land of the Scots, and leave the Borderlands to us. I wish to know the name of every person in your group, what your plans are, who is giving you direction, and when Robert the Bruce will return. I wish to know where he will attack first."

"I can't answer most of that." She lifted her chin a notch, showing her character, and locked gazes with him. The daring, deceitful bitch did not fear him.

That did not please him. He would change that.

He took a step closer until he was three hands away from her, her breath warming his chin. "What can you answer?" he whispered, their gazes locked. He had the sudden inkling that he may have just met his most formidable opponent. Strong of mind, especially for a woman, she would not bend easily. He stayed where he was, hoping his close presence would intimidate her enough to start talking. His hand reached out of its own accord to trace her jawline and then chuck her under the chin.

As he'd feared, she had the smoothest, silkiest skin he'd ever touched. Would the skin of her breasts be even softer under that tunic?

"I'll tell ye whatever ye wish to know as long as ye promise to set me free." Then she licked her lips, a slow movement of a tongue that he begged to taste, licking her lower lip in the most sensual display he'd ever seen.

It appeared to be a completely harmless movement, but something that set his mind to mountains of images, carnal, decadent images that would probably frighten her. That tongue of hers could prove to be very useful, and pleasurable, but he forced the images from his mind before he moaned and spent himself in his breeches.

"You'll tell me what I wish to know first. Then I'll decide whether it warrants setting you free."

"And if I dinnae do as ye ask?" That haughty little chin came up another notch.

"Then you'll lose one piece of clothing for each question you refuse to answer. As you can probably guess, once you are stripped of all, then I have access to all your delicate skin, and I promise to leave you marked as mine. I'll have the distinct pleasure of choosing the right spot."

"And then ye will take my maidenhead, I'm sure." She crossed her arms, pursed her lips and glared at him, the haughty, spoiled lass. He'd prefer to teach her a lesson or two over his knee. What man raised his daughter to be so bold, so tempting?

So sinfully desirable?

"Nay. Never. I would never do that to any lass. Your maidenhead is for your husband only. Even I have limits." He waited, refusing to step away as a small power battle took place between them, both refusing to step back. Instead of moving, she lifted her chin another notch as if to threaten him. Her neck had to be bothering her at this point.

"I'll start with your name. What is it?"

"That I'll tell ye. Reyna, daughter of the laird of Clan Matheson. Granddaughter of Logan and Gwyneth Ramsay, but I think ye knew that."

The twinkle in her eye lit up her entire face, bringing a light flush to her cheeks that were already a wee bit golden from the sun, something he rarely saw on a lady's skin. He approved.

"My turn," she said haughtily as if she deserved a turn.

"You do not gain a turn." He paced in a circle, thinking of all that could happen from here.

"Who are ye?"

He stared at the ceiling wishing he could tell her the truth, but he could not. "Who do you think I am?"

"Are ye the Wolf of the English garrison?"

He spun around to face her. "Ah, you have heard of me. I am surprised. I thought my reputation only carries in England. The Scots have heard of me? I'm flattered. And the full name is Wulfstan de Gray. You may call me Wulf."

He smiled just as a knock sounded at the door. "Dammit. I hate being interrupted." Wulf strode over to the door, opened it, and stepped outside. The messenger spoke loud enough for her to overhear.

"There is someone here to speak with you, Captain."

"About what?"

"He says it's about your sire."

Nothing else could have removed him from this chamber, but he had to see what the message was. It could be information that he'd waited a long time to hear.

He had to go.

"I'll be right there." He stepped back inside and grabbed a key on the wall. "I will return shortly with your evening meal. I will lock the door from the outside. Do not waste your time trying to get free."

He left without another word, taking the stairs as quickly as he could.

He hoped the bastard was dead, but he doubted he would be that lucky.

———— ❧ ————

Reyna hopped onto the bed as soon as she heard the key in the lock. She was exhausted and tired of playing word games with Wulfstan de Gray. A sigh burst from her lips of its own accord because the bed was as soft as any she'd ever been on, as soft as her bed at Eddirdale Castle and certainly better than the ground.

The chamber was far better than a dungeon. There was a hearth on the opposite wall with two chairs nearby and furs over the backs of the chairs. A full basket of wood sat off to the side. A table and three chairs sat on the back wall next to a chest covered with goblets, mugs, and eating utensils. There was a large pot to be hung over the fire in the hearth, but it was not in use presently. Perhaps she would be well fed too.

Reyna's eyes drifted shut, thinking this could be the best time for her to sleep. She rolled on her side and fell fast asleep after covering herself with the fur at the end of the bed. She dreamed of a man with long dark hair and ice-blue eyes standing at the end of a long path. She chased him, trying to reach him.

When she finally neared him, she stood as close as she could, staring into his beautiful eyes. Once she touched him, he turned into a wolf, his eyes turning green, his face brown fur, his teeth sharp, and his head tipped back in a growl.

She screamed, waking herself from the horrid dream.

Not surprisingly, when she bolted up on the bed, Wulf stood at the end, his hands on his hips. "I've been trying to wake you up. Get out of bed, go through the chest over there for a change of clothing or anything else you wish to take with you."

"Where am I going?" A bad feeling bubbled up her throat, the acidic taste burning her mouth.

"*We*. We are going to York, and we're leaving immediately. If you have needs to take care of, do it before we leave. I'll not be stopping."

"Why? What's in York?" she asked as she flung open the drawers in the chest, surprised to find some leather hair ties, a chemise, and a brush which she grabbed. There was also a soft tunic and a few other delicates.

He tossed her a small sack and said, "Whatever you choose, it must fit inside this."

She would squish what she could inside the sack.

Including the small dagger she found.

He stood at the door. "Hurry."

"What is the hurry? Why are we leaving?" Her gut wrenched because this would definitely affect her chance of being saved. Her group wouldn't think she'd gone to York. They'd search for her in Berwick.

Wulf shook his head, and she could see how

upset he was by whatever information he had received. Was it the entire garrison moving or just the two of them? She hoped it would be the entire army. That much her friends would notice and it definitely would make her location easier to trace. But he wasn't forthcoming with the news he'd received.

"You do not need to know why or where. Prepare to be gone for a few days. Change of clothes, night rail, whatever you can find in this chamber that will suit you, we will take." He grabbed her arm and dragged her to the door. "We leave in five minutes. I will return for you within that time. Do not delay me."

For some odd reason, Wulf's eyes had nearly changed to green. That couldn't be. She was turning daft. But she didn't have time to think on it.

As soon as he left, she searched the chamber for anything that could benefit her in York. Fortunately, her grandmother had always sewn folds on the inside of their tunics for the most important items to take on long journeys. Inside hers was a small container of two different poultices, a small, sheathed dagger, and a potion. She also carried a couple of linen squares and some dried meat in case they were taken captive or lost.

She packed a thin gown she found in one chest as well as an extra tunic and trews. Though they were clearly a lad's, she didn't care. Her bag was well-packed though she wished she still had her quiver, but that was not to be.

Either way, she had two daggers and food to survive.

Would it be enough to survive captivity with Wulfstan de Gray, the man with the reputation of being the cruelest man in the English garrison? Isla and Grif had both suffered, but they'd been saved by Dyna and Steinn within two days of their capture.

How could that happen to her when she was headed to York?

## CHAPTER FIVE

WULF TOSSED HER up on the stallion, mounting behind her quickly. He nodded to Emmot, the only other one he was taking along with him, that they needed to move through the burgh as fast as they could.

The messenger had told him that his father was moving more quickly than previously reported and that Tryana was betrothed, her wedding scheduled for the end of the week. Wulf needed to move quickly if he were to arrive in time to stop the marriage.

His plan was to get to York in a day and a half, then free his sister before returning to Berwick. He did not tell anyone why he was leaving, instead just putting one of his men in charge, claiming he followed orders to travel to London, saying he'd return in less than a sennight. There was little going on in Berwick, so he was not concerned about his absence.

It was a lie but a necessary one. Wulf wished he hadn't kidnapped the woman when he had. The journey would have been easier without her, but he couldn't undo what he'd done. And to leave her behind would probably cause her death with so many randy soldiers inside the castle. The only other alternative was to leave her with someone he trusted. Since there was no one that qualified for that, he had no choice but to bring her along.

Emmot followed, also bringing a third horse along with them. How Wulf hoped this would be a quick trip.

Nothing would stop him from finding his sire. The cold-hearted bastard. Tryana was nine and ten, very timid and beautiful. He feared she was betrothed to a cruel man like their father and he would not let his sister come to the same end as their mother.

Wulf had to protect his sister. It was his duty to make sure she wed someone worthy of her sweet nature. His mother would be counting on Wulf to watch over Tryana.

Once they were out on the path to York, the road was nearly deserted. It was nearly dusk and they'd be forced to stop soon. Anxious though he was to catch up to his father, he knew Wrath de Gray was a man of habit: He would stay in the same inn, eat the same food, and travel to the same shops once he arrived. He would not be hard to find.

"Your name again?" he asked the lass seated in front of him. She was related to the Ramsays, belonged to the Matheson chieftain, that much he recalled, but he didn't recall her first name.

She said nothing.

"Here is the situation if you choose to be a fool. You will tell me your full name, and we will travel as husband and wife. If you do not do as I ask, I will shave your head and carve my initials on your face." It was an empty threat. He'd never harm her, but he counted on her fear of him and his reputation as the Wolf to keep her compliant. He would never carve his initials on her face, but she didn't need to know that. He had to get her to travel with him so he could take care of the issue with his sire, then they could go back to being enemies.

"I'll be quiet on one condition. Will we return to Berwick after ye find yer sire?"

"Those are my plans." He'd never tell her his true plans, but that was enough to gain her acquiescence.

He gave her a minute to think on what he said but decided to add. "We will travel as husband and wife, but we will not sleep in the same bed. I will not force myself on you, nor will I allow any other men to take you with force."

"I agree." She sat with her back as straight as an arrow, not touching him unless forced to fall back against him, something he quite enjoyed. Something about this woman was different from any other he'd met. Proud, defiant, strong. Unlike his sister, who was meek and mild-mannered. He had no doubt that this woman would carve her initials on his face if given the chance. How did one raise a woman to be as such?

He looked forward to the challenge of determining just how clever she was, or if her pride was false.

"Now that we have an agreement, allow me to start again. Your name?"

"Reyna Ramsay."

"I thought your mother was a Ramsay."

"She is."

"Then Ramsay is not your name. Who is your sire?"

"Marcas Matheson. But I'd prefer to be known as a Ramsay in England. They probably know my dearest Grandmama."

"Reyna, the woman who looks regal enough to be Queen of the Ramsays. They should give you the title. You would wear it well, Reyna Matheson. I'll call you the queen of the savage Scots."

She said nothing, but he watched a flush rise up the back of her neck and he knew she was blushing like a young maiden.

Then he reminded himself that she was a young maiden.

They arrived at the inn, and he dismounted, helping her down as though they were married. He stepped close to her, inhaling her scent that nearly drove him mad on horseback. She smelled of everything good in the world, pine trees, mint, sunshine, and a bit of a flower, though he had no idea which one it would be.

If he weren't chasing his father, would he be chasing her?

Hardly fitting as his captive. He nearly snorted at that thought, but he restrained himself. "Come." He held his hand out to her. "I'll find us a chamber for the night." There were others about, so they gave the appearance of a young couple.

He held the door for her and then followed her in, leading the way to the innkeeper. "We'd like two chambers for the night. Have you two?"

"Aye, we do. We have two of our finer rooms available, both in the middle of the corridor above stairs across from each other. Will that suit you?"

"Aye," he said, handing the innkeeper the amount he requested for the stay.

"We'd like supper. What have you?" His gaze perused the few patrons in the dining part of the inn, looking for anyone who might cause him trouble, but he didn't see any obvious threats. It was the only inn for a ways, but there were many more in York, which was less than a day away. This establishment was clean, and the food was good. He knew that much from experience.

"My lord, we have beef stew or vegetable pottage. Bread and a berry tart."

"We'll have the stew, the bread, and a berry tart. Please bring enough for the three of us to our chamber."

Emmot said, "I'll take care of the horses and return in a short time."

Another group of three men came in after Emmot left, standing directly behind them. They appeared to be merchants, so he ignored them.

The three did not ignore Reyna. They stared at her, unable to take their eyes from the beauty. He had the feeling that Reyna knew she was pretty, but did she know how truly stunning she was? He doubted it, but she was about to find out.

"Saints above," one whispered to the other. "I swear she's the prettiest I've ever seen."

"She is, without a doubt."

Wulf leaned toward her and kissed her cheek, casting a glare at the men behind him.

Wulf tugged on Reyna's hand, returning his attention to the innkeeper. "Excuse us, so we may take our leave. If I stay, I'll repay the rudeness of your patrons, and I do not think you would appreciate the blood on the floor." The innkeeper rushed around to do as he was bid, not daring to make eye contact with either one of them. Wulf made a point to glare at the daft fools behind them one more time, lest they thought they would have any chance with Reyna. The innkeeper led the two of them above stairs, then opened the two doors, allowing Wulf to inspect the chambers and deem them acceptable. "These will be fine. We'll await our food in the next hour, if you please."

The innkeeper nodded and took his leave, hurrying down the staircase.

He opened the door for her and pointed to a chair next to a table with three other chairs. It was close to the fireplace where the embers of a banked fire glowed in the hearth. Wulf took care of the wood and soon had the fire burning again before he turned his attention to the rest of the chamber. There was a large canopied double bed with curtains around it, the table and chairs near the hearth, two chests with pillows atop one, and a basket full of blankets and furs next to the hearth. A screen stood on one side of the bed, meant to separate the sleeping area from the rest of the chamber.

Reyna could change behind the screen.

A knock sounded at the door and Wulf opened it impatiently. One of the merchants stood outside the door. "Is she taken? If not, I would like her. Miss, I'll marry you and take you back to my land near the border." Rather than wait for Reyna's answer, the fool held his palm up to Wulf. "I have good coin for her."

"She's taken. Get out." He didn't mince words. Spinning on his heel after he slammed the door in the fool's face, he stepped across the room and found himself less than a hand away from Reyna. Something in her face made him freeze.

Hellfire, but he couldn't stop his insane desire to stare at her any more than the fools at the door. Her green eyes caught his with a mix of emotions playing out in front of him. One was sheer anger at being held for so long. The other was a bit of fear, something he hated to see but would continue to use to his advantage. But there was more, though he wasn't sure exactly what.

Another knock at the door interrupted his thoughts. He moved over to open it, surprised to see the same man standing there. The man who dared to ask to buy Reyna. He cleared his throat and said, "Your pardon, but I will double the coin for her. I wish to marry her, keep her with child for the next several years."

Reyna bolted out of her seat and shouted, "What do I look like to ye? Something you can have just because ye like the way I look? Do I look like a cow to take home and milk for yerself? Do ye care to know anything else about me or just how pretty I am? Ye're a fool!" Wulf held his hand up to stop her tirade.

He grabbed the man by the collar, something that was easy because he towered over the little man. "If you knock on this door again or take one step closer to my wife, I will have ten men tie you to the ground and slowly cut you to pieces until there is enough blood to draw the vultures to suck your insides out."

The man's eyes widened, and he muttered, "Your pardon." Once Wulf let him go, he raced down the passageway and nearly fell down the staircase.

Closing the door again, he turned to find the fiery woman standing behind him, still upset. "Ye would think I was a piece of cooked meat on a table at the market." Reyna paced, still fuming over the audacity of the man. "Or am I just something to carry bairns for the rest of my life? I have a mind, or do none of ye men ever think on it? I'm capable of much more than lying on my back like a whore."

Caught off guard by her language, he wondered how she'd come to know of such things. How much did Tryana know of the expectations she'd have thrust upon her by her husband?

She stopped in front of him, the fury still evident on her face. She even wrinkled her nose a bit when she was angry, something he made a note of in his mind. It could prove useful someday. "And ye are just like him. Think ye that I am too mild-mannered, too protected, to know what a whore is? Well, I've traveled far, and I know more than ye think I do. My grandmother taught me the best thing to do was be strong and smart. That men dinnae know how to handle a smart woman. And she said 'twas easy to be smarter than most men. What say ye of that? Or do ye think my purpose is to bring bairns into the world?"

He couldn't stop himself. "Oh, you are far from that, my lady. Now if you had faith in me to protect you and keep your words to yourself, it would make things easier." His soft tone was meant to calm her down and intimidate her enough to sit again.

But she didn't. Nay, this woman was going to be a challenge unlike any he'd had forced upon him before.

She parted her lips, and he wished to thrust his tongue inside, tasting every part of her mouth. The deep green in her eyes mesmerized him, but she held her own, not saying a word. Grateful she hadn't begged someone to save her yet, she was being much more agreeable than he would have guessed. Arguing with the beauty was far better than tears, in his mind.

"But I do thank ye." She startled him, offering her thanks for not selling her to the odd man. "I dinnae know how to thank my abductor for not sending me away, but somehow, I believe my life with that man would have been worse."

The heat from having her so close began to build inside him, the need for release of his physical needs forcing him to think of ways to satisfy those needs. Even though it went against his moral ground to force himself on Reyna, that didn't mean he couldn't fantasize about how good they would be together. How sweet she would taste. How soft her skin would be.

How good it would feel to bury himself deep inside her.

And just like that, his erection pained him, begging to be set free of his trews. Standing this close to her was nearly orgasmic for him. He reached up and touched the back of his fingers to her cheekbone, and she jumped back as if he'd burned her.

So much for mutual attraction.

He stepped back, furious with himself for losing control. He was always in control.

Always.

Damn this woman.

# CHAPTER SIX

REYNA'S BELLY CHURNED with emotions she didn't understand. Standing so close to Wulf had upset her—upset her balance, her weakening control, her need to find a man.

She liked being so close to such an attractive man. Yet at the same time, knowing that he'd taken Isla captive made her wish to put her dagger into his heart. She didn't think this was the right place to do it.

If she killed him, who would protect her from the fools in the tavern?

She kept her words inside, doing her best to deny the physical attraction. Forcing herself to try to understand that when his skin touched hers, it was as if a bolt of lightning shot through her. This was her enemy, her abductor, one who she should hate, yet she was attracted to him more than any other man she'd met. She'd been drawn to him since she'd first spied him astride his horse as he'd approached Berwick Castle and as he'd chased her through the woods. She felt the longing for him unlike anything she'd ever felt before. She may have thought that she loved men in the past, but nothing compared to the feelings this man stirred in her.

But his reputation was terrifying, and just hearing his words about how he was going to torture that man made her realize that she needed to be careful with this man.

How could she hate him and be attracted to him at the same time? And how he'd kissed her cheek in the inn to claim her had caused a deep flutter in her belly. How he'd taken her hand to tug her close. How he'd barked at the man who'd asked to buy her for a wife.

He jumped back so quickly from her that she turned away, embarrassed by her simple reaction to his proximity. How could she explain to him how new this was to her? That no man or lad had ever stood that close to her once she'd grown past ten winters old.

She was the daughter of the laird, and as such, no man was allowed close to her. It was probably still the same on Ramsay land. Her mother had remarked how she and Jennet had both fallen in love with the men who kidnapped them. Tara too. How they'd been so restricted on Ramsay land they had barely shared a kiss with anyone.

Well, she'd been kissed, but not much more than that.

His words came over her shoulder. "If I had sold you to that peasant, he would have pawed you like an animal. You are a noble lady and should be treated as such. Barring my abduction of you, which I'll agree is not the best treatment, you must understand I had my reasons to do what I did. Everyone knows a noble person is far more valuable to hold in captivity. Your status gives me much more bargaining power."

Another knock sounded at the door, and Wulf answered it again, this time stepping back to allow a serving maid to enter, a man behind her, both carrying steaming serving dishes of stew and warm bread. One berry tart was also set on the table.

"Anything else, Captain?"

"That is sufficient."

The two left, and she took a chair, her belly rumbling from the smell of the food. She hadn't had warm bread since she'd left home. Wulf filled a bowl for her and handed her a piece of bread.

Embarrassed by how hungry she was, she slowed herself down, vowing to enjoy every morsel.

"My, you look as though you haven't eaten for days, Reyna." He took a mouthful of the stew and smiled at her.

She chewed on the bread, savoring the warm crust before she replied. "I have only eaten food on the road of late. I've been traveling for a while."

"For how long?"

"I was at Carlisle for as long as ye were, but we were in the forest, unlike ye." She stared at her food, not wanting to look him in the eye as he had the power to unnerve her, strictly because she found him so attractive. "I dinnae recall the number of days."

"Your instructions now that your king has gone to Ireland?"

She couldn't help but notice that he slid that question in as if they were best of friends. "We are here to keep watch over all the Borderlands, Berwick included. We have nae orders to attack. Just to keep an eye on ye." Telling him this much was nothing risky. This was something he could have guessed. She didn't feel that she'd betrayed anyone at all with this small bit of information. "My turn for a question. Why are we chasing yer sire?"

"You don't get a turn, my lady. It is no concern of yours."

"I think it is, my lord. Are you chasing him because ye plan on sailing off to Europe? Or are ye chasing him because ye miss him so much?"

His hand slapped down hard on the table. "Miss my sire? Never. I detest the man. Nor would I ever get on a ship with him."

"Ye hate yer father? I've been angry with mine, even more with my arrogant grandsire, but I've never hated either one. I love them. They gave me life," she whispered, wondering what could have transpired to have caused such a harsh reaction from him.

"He is incapable of any feeling, and he has my sister with him. I adore my sister. I chase him because I wish to know where they are going. If he's marrying her to someone, I need to know who it is and approve of the match myself." He stabbed a piece of meat with his dagger and ate it, scraping the metal blade with his perfect white teeth.

"Do that more often, maybe a little harder, then

I'll no' have to worry, will I?" She couldn't hide her smirk, amusing herself with the comment that he would certainly not enjoy.

"You would like that, wouldn't you? Am I that bad a captor?" His gaze narrowed as he focused on her, sending another set of butterflies through her insides.

"How would I know? I've never been kidnapped before."

"You are not kidnapped. You are abducted. There is a difference." He tore off another hunk of bread a bit too vigorously, telling her she'd hit a nerve. Perhaps she'd play with the man's temper. He said he'd never hurt her. Why not tease him?

"Nay, there is no difference."

"Aye, there is. Must you argue with me about everything, woman?" His eyes had a fire in them as he glared at her as if his expression alone dared her to continue.

"Ye are no' used to being questioned, are ye?"

He paused, pushing his chair back until he balanced on the two legs. "I am not. I am not accustomed to being ordered around, and I am accustomed to giving orders, but no one questions my orders." He let his chair down with a bang as if putting an exclamation mark on the end of his sentence.

"I think ye best get accustomed to my questions." She coyly lowered her eyes, knowing he was studying her before he spoke.

A knock sounded at the door, and he bellowed, "Enter, Emmot."

Emmot came inside with a smile. "Lovely evening."

"Here is your food. Kindly take it across the hall and eat by yourself. I'm nearly finished and when I am, I'll come over."

"Aye, Captain." He nodded, picked up his food, and left.

Reyna looked at the fruit tart and couldn't wait one minute longer. It fit her hand perfectly, so she bit into it, moaning involuntarily once she tasted the sweet pastry. "Oh my, this cook is excellent."

Wulf's gaze locked onto hers, but he said nothing.

"Would ye like a bite?" she asked innocently.

His eyes darkened, but he barked, "I would not."

"Too bad, but I'm glad. I'll keep it for myself." She smiled, waggled her brow at him, then took another bite, moaning again as the flavors assaulted her senses so wonderfully that she hardly noticed the dribble of frosting floating over her lip and down her chin.

Wulf jumped out of his chair. "Must you be so crude?"

"Crude?" She jumped, grabbing the linen square to dabble at the juice on her chin, but then she stopped herself. "'Tis too good to waste on a piece of linen." Instead, she used her tongue to catch as much of it as she could before sitting down again.

And Wulf's gaze followed her tongue as if it were the King's prize made of gold. She contained her surprise, the sudden power he just gave her overpowering her insides with joy.

Sheer joy.

He was uncomfortable. Truth, he was, so much that he bolted out of his chair and turned his back to her, repositioning himself as he strode to the other side of the chamber.

"My lord, is something wrong?" she asked as innocently as she could. She knew what was wrong. He'd gained an erection from listening to her moan and watching her lick the frosting from her face. She'd had no idea that her tongue held that much power, but she'd be certain to remember it. The use of it could come in handy.

"Nay, carry on. Finish your food. I am full." He stood by the window, opening the shutters to look outside, wanting to be sure she had no idea what she'd done to him, his most intimate desires betraying him in his breeches.

"But this pastry is luscious. The icing, the fruit squishes with the sweetest juice."

"Enough hearing about your food. Where did you learn to be so rude?"

"Rude and crude. Hmm. Is that no' unusual?"

She kept her laughter inside only because she was delighted that she now had the ability to control him.

He spun on his heel and said, "I'm going to visit Emmot."

Watch and learn.

She'd heard the men talk of such power a woman could have, but they had often said it was a rare female who knew how to use it.

Her mother had once told her that most women held a power they never understood and, thus, never used.

She'd asked her mother, "What power?"

"It doesnae matter now. 'Tis a power that grows from inside a woman. But when ye gain it, learn it, and use it well. Ye will be shocked to see what it can do for ye."

She had an inkling she'd just gained it and learned it.

Now it was up to her to use it well.

And she would.

## CHAPTER SEVEN

ULF THREW THE door open to Emmot's chamber.

"Is something wrong, Captain? Can I be of assistance?" He stopped eating and used the linen square to wipe his mouth.

"Nay, I will bear the brunt of the rude woman's comments. I will not subject you to such torment." His hands settled on his hips as he paced the chamber.

"They are talking about her below stairs. They are all hoping she goes below so they can gawk at her again. She is a fine beauty." Emmot broke his hunk of bread and began to chew rather loudly. Why was everyone annoying him so?

"She is. I hope no one is planning something foolish." Hell, but if he'd known she would be so hard to protect, he might have changed his mind about absconding with the wench.

"Like kidnapping her?"

He froze in his spot. "Is that supposed to humor me, my friend, because it does not."

"Nay, forgive me." Emmot returned to his food. Smart man.

He didn't care for the idea that there were others looking for her, others admiring her beauty, her innate sensuality. "I suppose I'll need to sleep in front of her door to protect her."

He heard a noise outside, so he bolted over to the door and threw it back. Two men, clearly sotted, stood in front of her door with a grin. "What the bloody hell do you think you are doing?"

"We're going to tell the pretty one that we love her. And we'd like a turn each with her. We'll pay good money for her."

Wulf wished he had his sword but he'd left it in her chamber, more evidence of how she'd unsettled him. He'd be lucky if she didn't use it against him. "Where is…" Then he saw Emmot's weapon, grabbing it and going out of the chamber toward the men, who took one look at it and ran back to the staircase. The fools shoved at each other so much that they both stumbled at the top and rolled down the stairs, hitting hard enough that they would remember it, even though they were so sotted they'd probably have no lasting effects from it.

He glanced down at the bottom to make sure they both got up. They did, chuckling. "Look, he wishes to kill us over a lass," the one said pointing at him.

"Nay, I'd just like to cut your bollocks off and feed them to you." One man laughed harder while the other one paled and took off out the inn door. "Or perhaps I will hang them over the entrance to the inn as a warning to others."

Shaking his head, he headed back to her chamber just as she opened the door. "Close that door!" he shouted.

Emmot opened his and then slammed it shut. "Not you, Emmot."

She didn't close the door. He marched over and stood so their toes nearly touched. "Do not disobey me, my lady." He ground the last two words out between a clenched jaw. Hell, but she was a challenge.

Sweat beaded on her face, but he said nothing. He hoped her reaction was as physical as his own. She licked her lips, dropping her gaze, but then lifted it again as if to challenge him.

"What happened?" Her voice came out in such an innocent drawl that he wished to call her bluff. This lass may have her maidenhead, but she was far from innocent.

"Nothing that is your concern. Go inside, and I will follow you."

How he prayed, she would move quickly so she wouldn't feel his traitorous member, which had begun saluting her beauty as soon as she ran that tongue over her lips.

She did as he asked this time. He stepped in behind her and retrieved his sword before giving his last instructions for the night. "Go to sleep on the bed. I will sleep on the floor in front of the doorway so no drunken fools will bother you."

"That seems…"

"Appropriate. I am tired, and I fear I will not sleep well. Please do as I ask, and I will see you in the morning. We will break our fast and head to

York. We should arrive before nightfall easily." He sighed and stepped back into the corridor, taking the dirty dishes with him. "Sleep well, my lady."

She nodded. She turned to him, the full-mounded breasts heaving with each breath as she stared into his face. "When will I be able to leave your chambers?"

The words were uttered with such coldness his knuckles turned white on the handle of the dagger. Wulfstan took another step forward, his heart pumping hard in his chest. "When I say."

She turned her back on him, her arms crossing over her chest as she stared at the fireplace. "I'm tired of being locked up. Will ye lock me up in York too?"

Then he opened the door and said, "Lock this. Do not open it for anyone but me."

She did as he ordered this time, to his surprise, but when she moved closer, he could see that she was as tired as he was. She now had dark circles under her eyes that he hadn't noticed before.

She closed the door and he listened to the lock, but then he had the sudden urge to break it open. It was entirely possible that the wench would try to climb out the window and steal a horse before running away, but she looked more exhausted than he was.

He had the odd feeling she understood how much danger she would be in if she traveled alone. She was headstrong, but she wasn't foolish. She'd seen the stir her presence had caused below stairs, seen the sotted men joining together to pay for her services. Riding down a busy path alone would not be a wise choice, especially when her beauty was not the kind one could hide.

Her curves, her green eyes, even the way she carried herself would attract a man's eye.

He'd had no idea that she was going to be so enticing when he'd abducted her. Oh, he could drum up multiple reasons for why he'd caught up with her and snaked his arm around her waist, but he knew the true reason. If anyone asked, it would be easy to lie and say he'd meant to give himself leverage with Robert the Bruce, and that he'd also hoped to gain the approval of his commanding officers.

But the true reason he'd done it was pure curiosity and lusty desire, and it bothered him that he was so controlled by his traitorous member. She'd caught his attention for other reasons, but the reason he'd acted on his thoughts engorged every time he was in her company.

Blast it, but he hated to be so weak, and he'd never admit it to anyone.

He'd spent so much time focusing on her beauty that he'd ignored the other pressing issues. He'd walked out on his garrison with little thought to justifying his actions. His fear for his sister had propelled him to act hastily. He hoped that having such a valuable captive would help him in the event that he faced any trouble for leaving the garrison. He hadn't been concerned earlier in the day when he made his hasty decision to go to York, but as time passed, he managed to have some second thoughts. He was a captain in the English army, and if he failed in his duty, they would not take it lightly. All he had to do was keep her alive, make sure his dear sister was safe and betrothed to a kind man, chastise his sire for his sins, then go back to Berwick.

This was going to be a difficult journey between the three subjects fighting for his attention—his father and sister, the English army, and a woman who was as pleasing to the eye as any he'd ever met. This was destined to be a test of his abilities, of his loyalties and skills.

Which one would he fail?

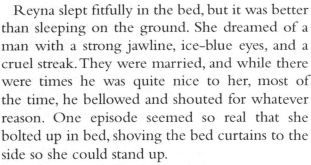

Reyna slept fitfully in the bed, but it was better than sleeping on the ground. She dreamed of a man with a strong jawline, ice-blue eyes, and a cruel streak. They were married, and while there were times he was quite nice to her, most of the time, he bellowed and shouted for whatever reason. One episode seemed so real that she bolted up in bed, shoving the bed curtains to the side so she could stand up.

She wished to vanquish the man from her mind, the man who abducted her on a whim and turned her life upside down with nary a care. Forcing her breathing to slow down, she finally understood what had awakened her.

Wulf was speaking to someone in the passageway.

She moved over to the door and leaned her ear to the wood, hoping to pick up all the conversation instead of his bellowing.

"Please, can we not just touch her? I'll just feel

her hair, her titties. I promise not to touch her skin beneath her clothing."

She had the sudden urge to remove the night rail she'd found in one of the chests and don her tunic and leggings again.

Another voice said, "She'll never know we're in the chamber. We'll not say a word, just watch her and touch lightly. I have plenty of coin. Whatever you wish."

Wulf's voice came out in such a deep threatening tone that she wished to warn the men that he was about to go over the edge. He roared, "Get your arses back down the stairs. No one touches her, no one goes inside." This time Wulf's voice was a low rumble. "Leave now, or I'll use my weapon on both of you. Then I'll cut out your tongues when I have you flat on the floor, just so you'll not ask again."

Wide-eyed, she turned her back against the door, her palms flat against it in case anyone tried to open it. It was locked, of that much she was certain. But she could not allow anyone inside. Scanning the chamber for her daggers, she feared she could pass out in fright soon enough.

The steps receded, and she let out the breath she'd been holding.

The next group came but a few moments later. "You have no trouble scaring two sotted men away, but my friends and I are not sotted. We have weapons. We want the lass, so give her up."

Wulf laughed at them, something they didn't approve of. She could tell the men were coming closer, but Wulf said nothing. Had he left her?

Her fear forced her to do the most ridiculous thing ever. She unlocked the door, knowing it was the wrong thing to do, but she had to know if she'd been left to her own cunning. She opened the door enough to peek out with one eye.

"Close the bloody door!" His voice came out as loud as she'd ever heard it, so she did as he said and locked it, but it apparently started a scuffle.

What followed made her shrink against the door, her back sliding down the door until she sat in a heap on the floor, tears in her eyes. Shouts of pain, cursing, banging against the wall, men falling.

Reyna had no idea what was happening. Was Wulf winning or losing?

A wee voice inside her reminded her she should be ecstatic about what was happening. Her captor could now be dead on the other side of the door.

She would be free to go back to Scotland.

But how could she get past all these men who wished to touch her with just two small daggers for weapons? Tears misted her gaze, but she swiped them away, angry with herself for her weakness. Isla probably never shed a tear when she was in the dungeon.

Her mother had told her she and Jennet had been held captive more than once. Her mother had cried often, but Jennet had never shed a tear, instead coming up with crafty comments that served to frighten their captors.

Once, she'd convinced them all she was a witch and could cast a spell on them, curse them.

It had worked.

Her mind churned with any possible thing she could threaten the men with. Then she thought of it. There was some sickness that the prostitutes carried. What was it called? She thought back to all the times she'd heard the guardsmen talking in the keep or during the festivals.

What had they called it?

Wracking her brain, she came up with nothing, but the noise in the passageway had calmed down.

Had he survived?

"Wulf?" she whispered. "Are ye there?"

No response.

She wrung her hands, wondering what she should do next. But then she heard something. It was him.

"Go to sleep. They are gone, and I'm fine." The whisper was barely audible, but it was clear enough.

She stood, straightening her night rail.

"Do not dare to open that door again until the morrow."

"I won't."

She fell onto the bed and settled the furs about her again. Then she thought of it.

The pox. That's what they'd call it.

She'd tell all the fools she had the pox.

⚬⚬⚬

Wulf climbed the stairs with a package and a large bowl of porridge, while a lad entered behind him carrying a large steaming basin of water.

He knocked on her door and said, "It is Wulf."

Pleased she opened it quickly, he stepped inside

but froze when he saw she was clad again in the sinful tight leggings and tunic.

"Here," he said, thrusting the package at her. "I purchased two gowns for you to wear over that outfit that makes you look like a lad. You cannot wear that in York. The frocks are close to your size, I hope. Here is a bowl of porridge with honey along with a pastry." He set the two items on the table after she took the package.

"I'll leave you to prepare yourself. Be below stairs in half the hour. I'll be at the bottom of the staircase. If anyone bothers you, scream, and I will hear you."

He left, closing the door and waiting for her to lock it, which she quickly did. Then he yelled to Emmot. "Meet me below stairs in five minutes to break our fast."

Wulf moved down the stairs and into the dining part of the hall, his gaze scanning the area, looking for any man who was looking for trouble. Most held their heads as if the previous night's indulgences held a tight control on them.

Good, perhaps they'd leave Reyna alone. Emmot joined him, and they ate without much discussion, the entire hall a low rumble of movement and conversation.

Until it came to a swift halt.

His back was to the staircase, so he turned around, and he had a sudden idea what they were all gaping at—Reyna Matheson.

It was Reyna, but it was a Reyna he hadn't seen yet. It was a woman who looked like she belonged in the royal castle, the dark blue gown he'd bought her clinging to her curves, her hair deftly plaited in a manner that was more than becoming. Her skin luminescent and as clear as any he'd ever seen.

She must have slept well, of that much he was pleased.

As soon as the first chair moved back, he bolted out of his seat and approached her, his hand held out to escort her. He gave her a small bow to let the fools around him realize she was as worthy of respect as any queen.

And that she belonged to him.

Reyna was as stunning as any woman he'd ever seen, her high cheekbones sporting a few freckles from the sun. Royalty would try to hide such imperfections, but he found them tantalizing. Evidence of the woman who loved horseback-riding and excelled at it.

She was a woman of mystery.

"Come, we are ready to take our leave." He took her mantle and helped her with it, then grabbed her bag before leading her out the door, every man's gaze following her every move.

He even heard a small whimper of pain from one fool.

"Have you any needs before we leave?" he asked after they were clear of the dining hall.

"Nay, I am fine. Please hurry this journey so we can return to Berwick." There were no smiles for him this morning, nor for Emmot.

He understood. She was their captive, his prisoner, nothing she should be pleased about.

Emmot brought their horses and Wulf helped

her mount. By the end of the day, they'd be in York.

And so would his sire. How he wished he'd be given the one opportunity he longed for.

The chance to kill his father.

# CHAPTER EIGHT

REYNA PAID CLOSE attention to everything on the way to York. They arrived ahead of dusk, but the sun would be gone soon. She had made up her mind. This time she would escape. All she would need was a bow and a few arrows to protect herself, and she'd find her way back to the Borderlands.

Wulf stopped at an inn that was nicer and larger than the one from the previous night. If she were fortunate, perhaps she wouldn't have twenty men ogling her. He helped her down, leaving the hood of her mantle over her head. He didn't argue. This time she had a gown on, and that would bring more attention.

She'd leave the hood up since there was still a slight chill in the air.

"Emmot, go inside and ask about our horses. See if there is room inside their stable in the back. I'll wait for you."

Once Emmot took his leave, Wulf turned his attention back to her, and they were so close it unsettled her. It was as if he were hiding her from view. "My lady, I will treat you as nobly as if you were my true wife, and I ask that you act like my wife as well. A demure lady of noble breeding that you are. I have business with my sire, and I expect he is already here. Once that business is concluded, I will return you to Berwick, as promised."

His gaze locked on hers, the ice blue melting a wee bit as he asked for her acquiescence. She peered up at him, the strong jawline, the dark stubble, the dark hair that was askew from the wind, a look she found more enticing. So askew that she nearly reached up to fix the stray hairs, but she didn't, reminding herself that he was the enemy.

"What say you?" he whispered in her ear, the heat of his breath traveling straight to her core, but she forced herself to ignore it.

"Will you set me free when we arrive back in Berwick?" She doubted he would agree to that, but it was worth asking. Even if he didn't, her chances of being found by Dyna, Maitland, and the others were much stronger if she were in Berwick and not York.

"Nay, not until your king returns. I wish to bargain with Robert the Bruce. I am confident he will do as I wish in return for your freedom. So your freedom depends on his timely return from Ireland. And whether you hold any value to him. Do you?"

She blushed at the question. King Robert the Bruce had no idea who she was. He would surely know her father's name, her grandfather and grandmother's name, and so many others, but

Reyna Matheson was only well-known on Black Isle. But he would bargain for her because of her grandsire, wouldn't he? Perhaps Maitland could convince him of her value. Whether it happened or not, she did not like discussing her value with this man.

"And what is it that ye wish to bargain for?" She stood nearly on the tips of her toes to gaze into his blue eyes again, and he paused, taking in all of her. It made her feel as if he undressed her, and an odd heat coursed through her. Had she ever held a man's attention as much as Wulfstan's?

"That is not your concern. I want nothing more from you than your value as a bargaining chip. If your king gives me the information I am seeking, then I will release you. It is that simple. Until then, why not do our best to get along?

She couldn't argue with his reasoning, so she instead took in all of her surroundings. They'd turned at the last crossroads to the left onto this bustling street, full of horses and people walking the street. A castle sat in the distance, but it was quite a distance away, probably overlooking the river if she were to guess. She stared at the ground for a moment, trying to build a map in her mind of the streets they'd passed once they came across the bridge into York.

The inn they stood in front of took up much of the street with a fine stone walkway and ornate carvings in the double door entrance. There appeared to be a large clientele breaking their fast inside, women and men, something she was glad to see. Here she would not be the only female.

The horse they'd ridden panted next to her, and she couldn't stop herself from leaning into the brown beauty, rubbing his withers with fondness.

She always knew what to expect from her horse—loyalty, love, and a wonderful ride. She had no idea what to expect from this man that held her captive, except for this unusual heat that coursed through her whenever his gaze locked on hers, or when he stood close.

That heat was something she guessed only a certain handsome man had the power to bring to her. That bothered her more than anything. He was her enemy. She'd heard her mother talk about how she'd fallen in love with Marcas Matheson. He had stolen Jennet and Brigid from their castle and brought them to Black Isle to save his clan. Her mother swore she'd been drawn to him from the very first moment their gazes had locked.

Was this the same thing? He was her enemy, her clan's enemy, Scotland's enemy. How could she find anything about him appealing?

She couldn't argue with his reasoning, and thus far, he had been kind to her, protecting her when necessary. He'd even fed her well and gave her the bed to herself.

"My lady?"

She whispered, "Agreed. As long as we return within a few days. I make no promises after that."

His gaze traveled across her skin, nearly branding her it was so heated. "Fair enough."

Emmot exited the inn and said, "I'll take the horses around back."

"Good. See that they are brushed down and fed."

Emmot nodded and they stepped around the horses, making their way inside the heavy dark wooden doors.

No sooner had Wulf's hand reached for the door when a booming voice called out to him. "Well, well, well, if it isn't my waste of a son."

Reyna whirled around and saw who she presumed to be Wulf's father dismounting from his horse, another man next to him. Even if the man hadn't called Wulf son, she might have guessed it by the way Wulf tightened his grip on her elbow, squeezing it until she was nearly ready to scream. She glared at him, and he caught her unspoken message, letting up on the pressure from his hand.

"Since you do not deserve a greeting, I will not offer one. Where is Tryana?"

"It is no concern of yours." The man was not nearly as handsome as his son, his hair mostly gray and sparse in spots. His physique was not as tight as his son's either. He looked to be flabby underneath his clothing.

The strain on Wulf's face was something no one else would see but her. It was there for a fleeting moment before it disappeared, cleverly concealed again. "Since she is my sister, and I care for her far more than you, I'd like to know her whereabouts."

"If you wish more details, you can meet me in my chamber in half the hour. Until then, this conversation is over."

Reyna took the chance to study the town, knowing her captor was busy with his sire. First rule of her grandmama's—know your surroundings. She needed to study the town of York even more. Or was it a city? She had no idea, but it was busy. They had entered the town by a bridge across a river, though she had no idea its name. They traveled to something called Collier Gate, possibly? They paid a toll, but she couldn't hear the conversations closely, and she had trouble understanding the English at times.

From where they stood now, the street was remarkably busy. It was not a market street, but she noticed a shop for a goldsmith and one for a blacksmith. Beyond that, she was uncertain. They'd turned a corner to get to the inn, but the crossroad was not far. There was also a town stable visible down the street.

All she had to do was find a horse and follow the road back out of the city. Head straight north, something she could do easily as both her grandparents had taught her how to judge directions by the sun, a skill she would desperately need later today. She hoped to pass an armorer or any place where she could grab a bow and quiver and multiple arrows.

But where? And how? She had no coin.

Determined to escape, she gave little more attention to Wulfstan's sire, because she had no intention of ever speaking with him again.

Turning his back on his father, Wulf led her inside, stepping into the entryway and adjusting to the darkness. They moved to the end of the corridor where there was a desk, the innkeeper behind it, and the dining hall off to the right.

"We'll take your finest chamber and another small one," he said to the innkeeper. "Please be quick about it. You have more people coming in, and I do not wish to get slowed in our plans." Wulf turned around, watching for his sire if she were to guess. Arguing inside the inn would not fare well for either of them. But the fact that he was going to visit with his father gave her hope.

Hope that she would be given the chance to escape. She needed to stay alert, watch her surroundings, and take advantage of any situation.

The innkeeper replied, "Absolutely, my lord. I will have my lad lead you to your chamber. And here is the key to a smaller chamber at the end of the passageway before the second staircase to the outside. Would you like any food for your dining pleasure? There is a table in the larger chamber."

A second staircase to the outside was something important. That could be her escape route. Coming down the main staircase would be risky, but the back staircase should be safer because it was probably rarely used. Her heartbeat sped up at the possibility of escaping soon. She had to calm herself or he would notice.

"Please send whatever you have for the evening meal. Where is the lad?" He scanned the area but then grabbed her wrist to lead her away before jerking back toward her. He said nothing, just casting an odd look her way.

The man called out a name, and when the lad entered, he gave the boy the key to their chamber.

Wulf paid swiftly and nodded for the boy to lead the way. They followed and he had a tight hold on her hand as if he thought she would run away.

The boy led them to the wide staircase in the middle of the inn, a red carpet covering the center of the steps. Everyone could see them, something that made her uneasy. She went up the stairs ahead of him, glad that he'd finally stopped staring at her so oddly. But to her surprise, he stopped her at the top of the stairs. He leaned over and whispered in her ear, "Why is your pulse racing?"

She jerked her attention away from him, refusing to answer, her mind flying through possible explanations.

He moved her ahead of him as they followed the boy down the corridor, his hand at the small of her back. He paused and whispered again, this time a little softer and a little closer, his closeness unsettling her even more. "Could it be…"

She whirled her head back to face him, knowing this would be the only answer he would accept without question. "Mayhap I am attracted to ye and yer closeness affects me. Daughters of chieftains have little experience around men."

He couldn't stop the small smile from breaking out, but he ushered her to follow the boy again, and they walked in silence down one passageway to another. At least he'd stopped his inquisition.

They managed to be partway down the passageway before the sound of the front door opening carried to him, along with the abrupt tone of his sire's voice, bellowing his greeting to the innkeeper. "I'll take your finest chamber."

She caught the small smile on Wulfstan's face at the idea that he had bested his sire, if even in one small way. Keeping her thoughts to herself, she guessed he would wish to overhear all his father said to the innkeeper.

She couldn't help but wonder what had caused the estrangement between father and son. She probably would never know, nor did she care. She did not consider the man a threat.

The lad stopped at the door midway down the wide but elegant passageway, lit by multiple wall sconces, and used the key to let them inside. Wulf set her satchel on the chest near the door.

"Many thanks to you. Send the food up when it is ready," he said to the serving lad before he departed.

He helped her off with her mantle, then paced while she sat down. It wasn't difficult to guess his plans. He was waiting to hear what chamber his sire would be in. Would he then take his leave?

If so, she'd be escaping. This could be her only chance, with Emmot not around either.

Emmot had taken the horses around the back, so she presumed he was still in the stable. If Wulf left her here alone, it would be a perfect time to plan her escape because he would be preoccupied with the multiple issues with his sire. She took note of what she would take along, her satchel, her mantle, and if they brought the food up soon, she'd take a hunk of bread or cheese, whatever was available.

She had a long ride back to the Borderlands alone. True, she was young, but she was not afraid. She'd find a way out and make her mother and grandmother proud of her.

Patience, she needed patience.

A serving lass entered with a tray of food and set it on the table.

Behind the lass, Wulf's father was visible in the corridor, entering the chamber directly across from Reyna's. A smile crept across Wulf's face as he watched. Wulf gave the lass a coin, and she left, closing the door behind her.

Reyna perused the tray with two trenchers of some stew, a loaf of bread, and a small brick of cheese. There were two apples on the tray, also. She took one and set it near the satchel to hide in the fold of her trews later. Not easy to get to it with a gown over her leggings, but she'd find a way when necessary.

The serving lass took her leave, then Wulf held a chair out for her, so she sat, settling her skirts and still keeping an eye on her satchel not far from the door. Then she waited to see if he would serve her the way he had the night before.

Wulf took two bites of his stew, nodding his approval and motioning for her to try hers, so she did. It could be the only food she ate that day. After a third bite, she broke off two pieces of the cheese, eating one and leaving the other to hide in her sack.

Just as she'd guessed, he waited a few moments, then said, "Please excuse me for a moment."

He disappeared into the chamber across the

passageway, slamming the door after he entered.

Reyna did not have much time. She grabbed the cheese and the apple, stuffed both into her sack, then donned her mantle before heading out the door, leaving it open so he would not hear the latch close. She crept down the passageway to the back staircase the innkeeper had mentioned before, praying it took her straight out the side of the inn.

When her feet hit the bottom, she couldn't stop the sigh of relief when she opened the door and stepped out into the gray mist of the day, though dusk was nearly upon them. No one was about to see her, so she lifted her hood and hurried toward the town stable. She couldn't go in the back or she'd risk being seen by Emmot.

To her surprise, as she headed down the street she noticed a horse off to the side with no rider nearby. Oddly familiar, she recognized it as Wulf's father's horse because of the white mark between its eyes. Odd that it was still here, but if the stable lads were busy, it could be a while before they brought the beast into the stable behind the inn.

Considering it a fine stroke of luck, she decided to take it. She whispered sweetly in the stallion's ear, let him get her scent, patted his withers, then mounted him. With a soft neigh, they were off. All she needed was a bow and arrow.

She turned right at the crossroad and took the path back to the bridge, glancing over her shoulder to see no one was following. Up ahead, she noticed a horse with a quiver on the back, so she approached slowly. She saw no one paying her any mind, so she leaned over and grabbed the quiver, pleased to see a bow and arrows all tucked inside.

Once she reached the bridge, they crossed, and she took a brief moment to appreciate the view of the river, the sound of rushing water reminding her of Black Isle, her sweet homeland. Heading across, she reached the other side without anyone behind her and set the beast to a lovely gallop. Several groups were heading to the town, but very few heading out, which pleased her. They'd be coming closer to dusk, which wasn't far out.

After about half the hour, there were few on the path, so she took in the placement of the sun before it disappeared behind the horizon, and paid attention to her bearings as Grandmama Gwynie had taught her before heading straight north.

Off to the Borderlands she went, happy to see a few recognizable landmarks. She allowed her hood to fall and laughed in joy, leaning her head back when the sun popped out between the clouds, if only for a few moments.

That was her mistake.

A group of ten men came up from behind her, attempting to surround her, so she headed off the trail and into the forest, where she knew she could beat them. A few fell away quickly, but four others stayed directly behind her with plenty of hoots and hollerings.

When she reached a clearing, she clucked at the horse to stop so she could dismount. The four men slowed, and when one of them growled an animalistic growl, she quickly found her bow and took aim. She had several arrows. If she was lucky, she might get them before they got her.

The man with the largest sword moved fast, clearly the one in charge, while he barked out orders. The other three men started to surround her, so she stuck the leader with an arrow in his chest, then the one behind him who had just begun to run at her, catching him in the belly, dropping him to the ground as he writhed in pain, trying to yank the arrow out. The other two stopped and looked at the bodies, then at her.

She pointed at them and hissed, "Come on, ye bloody bastards!

They hesitated, then bolted.

She whistled, but the horse she had ignored her. If she only had her own horse.

But it wasn't to be. Reyna mounted and left the trail, heading back to the main path. She wasn't on it long before another group of men came at her. Hell, but this was going to be more difficult than she'd expected.

One man came up on each side of her while two others remained behind her. As she fought off one man with a kick, another approached from the opposite side and snaked an arm around her waist.

Captured again.

# CHAPTER NINE

WULFSTAN WAS FURIOUS with his sire, so he moved into his chamber as soon as he knew the bastard was alone. "Where is Tryana?"

His father took a sip from the goblet he held before he turned around to face him.

"Wulfstan, what are you doing here? And who is that whore you have with you?"

"She is not a whore but my wife. And you do not need to know her name. Again I'll ask. Where is my sister?"

The bastard shrugged his shoulders, a smug expression on his face. He enjoyed taunting his only son, the one who would normally inherit all he had.

Wulf wanted none of it.

He waited, crossing his arms and rubbing his chin to keep himself from planting his fist in the man's face.

His father took another sip of his ale, then replied, "She is with her betrothed at his home not far from here."

"Who? I want a name."

"What does it matter to you? You'll never see her again. He'll have her with child within a fortnight, and she'll never leave there again. Forget your sister. I have done my duty and arranged her marriage. She's there to serve her purpose, producing heirs."

Wulf closed the gap between the two of them, grabbing his father by the throat. "Where is she?"

"Fine, I'll tell you. She's betrothed to the Baron of Topcliffe, Gareth Ward."

"The one who killed his first wife?"

"Indeed. She gave him no bairns, so he beat her. Then she took her own life."

"You spineless bastard. What did we ever do to you to deserve such treatment? The only one you ever cared anything about was yourself. You disgust me." The curl of his father's lip told him everything he said pleased the beast. He let go of him and shoved him away. "You are not worth my time."

He moved back to the door and opened it slowly, wishing to say anything he could to hurt his father. "Ironic that the only one of us who ever returned your love was Tryana. And she's the one you hurt the most. What is in that muddled mind between your two big ears? Very little, obviously."

The goblet flew across the chamber aimed at his head, so he ducked out and slammed the door. The sound of the thud when it hit the door made him smile.

His father was so vain, especially when it

concerned his large ears that managed to stick out.

When he spun around, his belly flopped in a way he didn't like. The door was open to his chamber and the chamber was empty.

Where the hell was Reyna?

Reyna bit the arm of her attacker, and she hung on until she tasted blood. That turned her belly, so she let go, only to be caught by the fool's large paw as he struck her head from the side.

An odd sound rang in her head, the sound of pealing bells scaring her, but they diminished within a few moments.

"Bring her over here in the clearing. We can share her." A man with a protruding belly and no teeth pulled up along the side of them, his grin so sickly she nearly heaved off the side of the horse. Another came behind him.

"I want her too. We can take her all night long. Then we can leave her in a pile, and no one will ever find her in the woods. Just the animals."

She peered at each face, one uglier than the other, though Toothless was the worst. The one who held her didn't smell as bad and had most of his teeth, appearing young and stronger than she would have preferred. He barked, "You are not getting her. She's mine. I got her. I'm marrying her, and you can both leave us."

The other two argued with him, but she ignored him because she had to find a way out of this. What would her grandmother do? Her

mother? Isla? She would find a way out. Isla had
said she acted like she liked the man, then he'd
fallen for her trickery, allowing her to get close
enough to stab him. A dagger sat attached to his
belt on the back of his breeches, giving her an
idea. That weapon would be in her hand as soon
as they stopped.

Although if she did it now, she'd still have a
horse. The other mount, the one she'd been
riding, had disappeared into the woods.

Her voice came out in a near squeal. "He's the
one I want. Not you two, so get lost. Give us
some privacy."

Her captor liked her suggestion because he
gripped her waist with a squeeze and whispered
in her ear. "I'll treat you well, lass. We'll live in the
forest."

Then he looked at his companions. "Leave, I
said."

"Can we watch, Henry? I'll stroke myself off if
I could just watch."

She shook her head slightly, so her captor said,
"Hell, nay. Get away now. I'm going to make her
mine." The man was clearly delirious, but she'd
go along with him just to get him alone.

Get his weapon. Stab him. Get him off the
horse, and she'd get free.

Once the others stayed back, she waited long
enough to make her move without an audience.
She faced him and hugged him, feeling for the
dagger, pulling it out of its sheath and slipping
it inside the fold made in her mantle while they
rode. Carefully reviewing her choices, she leaned

against him, deciding it might be best to get a wee bit further away from the others.

Then once they dismounted, she could stab him, mount his horse, and head north.

He finally stopped, and her heart beat so fast in her chest that she thought she might heave.

He helped her down and took her hand, leading her into a clearing off the path. "I've never seen a lass as beautiful as you. Can you take that mantle off so I can see all of you?"

That's when he made his mistake. He reached for her and slipped his hand under her mantle to squeeze her breast. That one move he made set her insides into a fury, and she reacted instinctively. The dagger came out of its hiding place, and she gripped it, plunging it deep into his belly. The look in his eyes was one of shock, but she ignored him, backing away when he reached for her throat.

Her grip never let off on the knife until she stepped back, blood dripping from the blade. She nearly dropped it, but she knew she had to keep it. Her kidnapper fell backwards as his eyes rolled back in his head.

She did just as Grandmama had taught her—push deep in the belly and pull up to do as much damage as possible. Her heart beat so fast she thought she might pass out, but first, she had to get to that horse.

Cleaning the blade on the grasses, she then returned it to the fold in her mantle, hurrying back to the horse. She'd lost her sack and quiver, but she could still find her way. Leaving the clearing, she nearly reached the horse when she heard voices calling out.

"There she is. Get her!"

The bellowing scared the horse just as she mounted, and he took off in a mad scramble, running wildly, so unsettled that the rotten beast tossed her off to the side.

She hit the ground hard, and the wind was knocked out of her, making her suddenly unable to move. She reached for the dagger just as a group of five men jumped off their mounts and headed straight for her. Toothless was first to reach her. "She's mine first."

"Ye ugly brute, ye'll not be touching me." Barely able to stand, she swung at him and caught him between his legs, setting him off in a keening wail unlike anything she'd ever heard.

Four more came at her. The first fist connected with the side of her head and nearly knocked her out.

She begged for death.

# CHAPTER TEN

WULF RAN DOWN the passageway and into the dining hall, peering around but saw no women at all.

"You looking for your wife?"

He just stared at the innkeeper, unwilling to admit his failing. The man obliged him and said, "Just saw her on horseback heading toward the bridge. I'd gone to the buttery down the street when I saw her fly by."

Wulf hurried out and raced around back, catching sight of Emmot coming toward him. "She left. I'm going after her. You wait here in case she returns on some innocent journey."

Emmot acted quickly, readying Wulf's horse just before he mounted and grabbed the reins.

His mind jumped to a thousand places, but foremost was that she'd left him, and he had a sinking feeling deep in the pit of his belly. It was a feeling of loss—but this was a woman, a captive Scots woman at that. He'd agreed to take care of her when he'd stolen her away. Her death could be blamed on the English, but that wasn't the greatest fear that caused the choking sensation in his throat and his chest. It was more than worrying someone else would kill her. What was this odd attachment shooting through him? What had caused it?

He knew full well what had caused it, but he didn't wish to admit it. It was a person. Nay, a woman. A beautiful woman who he felt responsible for. But it was more than that, and he knew it.

Was this that ridiculous emotion others called love starting inside him?

He had no idea. Other than his mother's love, he had no knowledge of the simpering feeling. Wulfstan de Gray was too powerful, too strong, to need such an emotion in his life. Loving someone like Reyna Matheson would be foolish, making him vulnerable in so many ways he had to force himself to dismiss the feeling.

Except it didn't go away. In fact, the farther he went, the stronger the fear became.

He passed Collier Gate and headed toward the bridge that took him back over the river, not surprised to pass one man cursing and swearing in the middle of the street next to his horse. "Who dared to take my quiver?" He searched the area for any sign of a bow and arrow, but Wulf had an idea he knew exactly where that quiver was.

On the back of whatever horse Reyna had stolen.

Once on the other side of the bridge, he sent the horse into a gallop, taking the same path they'd taken into York. He traveled for half the hour without seeing any sign of her, but then he passed a sure sign she'd been here: His sire's horse chewed on grasses just off a fork in the road. Wulf dismounted, moving over to the beast to make sure it was indeed his sire's, and he found more than he'd expected. The saddlebag held a wee bit of food and a pair of leggings, but the quiver on the side convinced him that this was indeed the horse Reyna had taken.

Then where was she?

Wulf's heart sped up. Where had she gone? What would she do? Lost out there by herself in the middle of the forest in England conjured all kinds of fearful thoughts about where she could be. *Dear God, let her not be harmed.* His mind churned with the possibilities, but he could not come up with any thought that made sense to him. She was a lass alone in the wilderness. What would Tryana do? His sister was the only link he had to a lass Reyna's age.

He didn't know how long he stood staring at the satchel in his hand, but he was unable to move. His thoughts were caught in a spider's web, and he was unable to reason his way out of his panic. It had been so long since he'd felt like this—so long since he'd been so afraid. He took a deep breath, in and out, trying to force himself to think.

The horse sidled away from him and went back to grazing. He shook his head, then, forcing himself to focus. He had to find her. He had to know if she was all right. He rushed back to his mount and sent him off into the fork, the less traveled path, attaching her satchel to his saddle as he rode.

Pausing, he cursed himself for his indecisiveness, but he set his horse back to his sire's and reached over for the quiver, sighing when he took it and attached it to his horse's saddle. Giving the lass a weapon against him could be the biggest mistake of his life, but it could also protect the two of them against any men out there. He was decent with a bow, but better with a sword. But he couldn't do both at once.

Convinced he was on the right track, he moved along, hoping to find her though dark was settling on them. It wasn't long before he met a small group of men, though he'd guess them to be small-time thieves by their clothing and the horses they rode. Men of substance rode strong horses.

Not these men.

He stopped, hoping they'd not bother him since he still wore the clothing of nobility, his doublet of the finest wool and his boots clearly expensive. He unsheathed his sword to let them know he was armed and prepared to fight if necessary.

"Have you seen a lass riding alone? Dark-haired?"

One grinned and grabbed his crotch. "Aye, and she's getting a swivving that I wished I was giving her right now."

Two others guffawed, the three crudely describing exactly what they'd like to do with her. The fourth man remained serious, searching him up and down. "Captain or major?"

"Captain de Gray."

"If she's related to you, you will wish to hurry. Head down the path, and you'll find her, but it won't be pretty. And you do not have enough power to stop the three who went after her."

"Nay, it was only one, Horace."

"And three more swung back to try to watch, or did you forget, idjit?" He glared over his shoulder at the one who still had his hand on his crotch.

"My thanks to you. I'll be on my way." He moved his horse around them, making sure he was not within reach of any of them before sending his mount into another gallop. There were no signs of anyone following him, so he egged his horse on. Almost out of earshot, he heard one say, "I'm following."

The man with the common sense said, "His name was de Gray. Does that mean naught to you? The cruelest man in the army."

"Shite, I did not know that. I'll stay away from him. Never mind. Leave him be."

They didn't follow, so he gave a small smile and congratulated himself on such a wise plan. Most of the stories of his history were false, just built to scare off the fools of the world.

Forcing himself to concentrate, he moved forward, his gaze scanning both sides of the path for any sign of Reyna, but the forest was thick with lush greenery and various sounds of summer.

Birds chattered, bees buzzed, and small animals rustled through the leaf litter. It was difficult to hear the whisper of leaves over their fluttering, or any indication of someone moving in the distance.

He followed the trail deeper into the woods, until he passed the thick trunk of a white oak tree, its branches curving out in every direction. A sword sat at the base of the tree, but no one was in sight.

He continued, convinced she was nearby, until the atmosphere changed around him, the kick of dust visible ahead of him, the cries of pain and the sound of flesh hitting flesh caught him, and he was on alert.

Rounding a bend, he slowed his horse as soon as his gaze fell on the melee a short distance ahead of him. Unsure of the participants, he edged closer, then froze, his hand reaching to close around the hilt of his weapon, gripping it tightly.

The flash of the sun reflecting off a blade caught him just before Reyna stabbed a man between his legs, catching him square enough to send the man into a rant of pain that scared the mice in the forest into running away, he was sure of it.

Three other men went after her, one fist catching the side of her head, nearly knocking her out. A fury let loose inside of him that was totally unknown to him. He was used to fury because his sire was hitting or beating someone, but this was different. This was a fury of protection, of gut-wrenching fear. The fear of losing her was more than he could handle, nearly costing him his usual ability to handle every threat calmly and carefully.

He was not calm.

Wulf drove his horse straight at the group, his sword ready in his right hand, as he let out a loud yell to let her know he was coming. She fell back, and he struck the first man's arm, the one whose fist had dared to strike Reyna. His arm dangled at a sickly angle, and the three spun around to face him.

This time he dismounted, tossing the quiver at Reyna. "Get up and shoot. There are more coming."

He knew the bastards had followed him. Something had changed their mind. Lust.

Swinging his sword at the next man who dared to brandish his sad-looking sword, he struck him straight in his heart and the man crumpled to the ground. The third man growled and swung his sword over his head at Wulf, but he never connected, the strike to his belly disabling his swing just before Wulf ducked to miss the fall of the blade.

"Reyna, get up!"

She lifted her head, her hand against her face, but caught his gaze and pushed herself to her feet.

"You have to fight with me, lass. There are more coming."

Four more headed straight at them from behind, the men he'd thought he'd scared off with his name and reputation. It hadn't lasted long. The quiet one was no longer with them, but another had taken his place.

The charging riders were almost upon them, weapons at the ready, their horses stirring up so much dust that it was difficult for him to see. To his delight, an arrow sliced through the air and caught the leader in his chest, causing him to fall off the side of his mount. Apparently, her vision was far better than his.

But he didn't like that she was in the open, a place where the men could surround her. "Get off to the side so they cannot strike you, Reyna. Hide in the trees."

She did as he said, more nimbly than he would have expected, but she was behind bushes and climbing a tree in a few moments while he mounted his animal and waged a battle with the three remaining men. He took the one closest to him first, and with a well-placed slice across the man's throat, he caused the bandit to fall off his horse without a sound. The second man did not prove as easy to kill. He fought harder than the first, and twice he nicked Wulf's leg before Wulf was able to fell the man.

Reyna fired her arrows in rapid succession while he was occupied, but she was forced to make a difficult shot as the third man had aimed his small sword at her and almost hit her. He then turned back to Wulf, and their fight continued until the third man suddenly dropped his sword. Reyna had shot him in the back.

Panting from the rush of battle, Wulf turned slowly, looking for more attackers, but there were none. The two were dead, two had been injured, and the horses were long gone—except for his.

"Reyna, are you hale?" he asked, walking toward her, doing his best to slow his breathing.

She dropped from the tree and stepped out of the bushes, her clothing and hair both in disarray, but he saw no wounds other than the bruising on her cheek. God's teeth, but she was a beauty. She was stunning in battle. Her cheek had a shadow from where she'd been punched, and her plait was barely holding together, but she looked him square in the eye, her high cheekbones flushed, her pink lips plump with exertion.

A queen named Reyna. How appropriate.

Her gaze dropped to his leg, something he'd forgotten. "You've been stabbed."

"So I have."

He glanced down at his breeches, surprised to see a large amount of blood flowing from one of his wounds, the one well above his knee, the fabric sliced clear across and allowing the blood to flow freely. The other cut was merely incidental. But the higher one was deep and he pressed on it with his hand. How was he to stop it?

That didn't matter to him now at all. He was more interested in how long it would be before she stole his horse. As if she read his mind, her head turned to stare at the only horse left.

He settled his hands on his hips and said the words she wished to hear, though he didn't understand why. "Go ahead. You wished to go free. I cannot stop you now. Take my horse and head to the Borderlands. Godspeed, but please leave me the water skein." Had her tussle with the men changed her mind? Made her realize how unsafe it was for her out here alone?

The indecision bounced across her face as clearly as if she'd spoken the words. He wasn't going to fight her. It was solely her choice. She had to know she could be dead by the morrow.

Then he reminded himself how young and naïve she was.

"Why?" she whispered. "Why would ye let me go after all that has transpired?"

He shrugged, not willing to admit the truth. There were two things that were stopping him from taking her captive.

The first was strictly physical. He fought hard to maintain his dignity by continuing to stand. It wouldn't be long before he collapsed or passed out.

The true reason was such a glaring admission that he'd never tell another soul. Even Reyna.

The truth was he was falling in love with her, and her happiness mattered more than keeping her captive.

## CHAPTER ELEVEN

REYNA TOOK TWO steps toward Wulf before he collapsed in front of her. This was her chance. She could hop on the horse and head north, be in the Borderlands by the morrow. It didn't matter that he might not survive, or that he'd abducted her, that he'd dragged her all the way to York for personal reasons. Because of him, she'd nearly been molested, been attacked, and bruised. That's what happened to girls alone in the woods. Even her mother and grandmother had taught her that rule.

But he'd taken her from her Scottish patrol. He'd abducted her, risked her life, and coldly barked orders at her.

But he'd also saved her. Tears misted her eyes at the sad reality she found herself faced with.

She couldn't leave him. There was no way she could steal his horse and leave him here to die.

What the hell was wrong with her?

She told herself it was the healer in her that kept her from walking away because it was that knowledge from living around her mother and her aunts Tara, Jennet, and Brenna that gave her the skill and expertise that few had. The art of healing. Not just the art, but the compassion. She'd seen them help people they didn't know, ones who were rude and cruel and old.

That was surely the reason she would stay, because she was a healer. It had nothing to do with these warm feelings she had toward him. This squeeze on her heart when she thought of leaving him alone, wounded, bleeding. Hurting.

She could fix him. "Wulf, I'll no' leave ye yet. We need to get ye on the horse, then I'll lead him back to a burn we passed no' long ago. I could hear the water running so 'tis off the regular path but no' too far. I'll dress yer wound and get ye settled before I leave."

"You do not need to do that. I'm a member of the king's army. Someone will find me and get me back to York," he said, grimacing as the pain shot through him at the small attempt to stand.

"Here," she said, pulling his horse over and handing the reins to him. "Hold on to these on one side and I'll be on the other. Once ye are standing, I'll help to get ye onto his back."

After a wee bit of struggling, she managed to get him onto the horse, though she knew she did not have much time to waste. He was still bleeding too much from the one wound.

"How far back?" he asked, swaying a bit.

"Not far. We'll be there in less than a quarter hour. Press your hand down on the wound until we get there. Hard." She did her best to show him, but he didn't seem capable of absorbing much of her instructions at present. The sweat on his brow, the glazed eyes, the light panting with his breath sounds told her he was barely staying on the horse. There was no time to waste so she hurried the horse back to the side path she recalled because she also had to be alert to any more marauders.

They would not fare well if a group of reivers came upon them.

Once inside the clearing by the burn, she led the horse to a mossy spot not far from the bubbling water and helped Wulf to lean back against the tree. It would help him stay alert, and she needed him awake. She found the water skein and gave him a sip before filling it with fresh water and setting it at his side.

She held her hand out. "Yer dagger."

He locked gazes with her, and the intensity of his gaze shocked her. It was entirely different than what she'd witnessed before. His hair was quite curly at the bottom from all the activity, the disarray only adding to his handsome looks. But it was the expression in his gaze that stilled her. Wulf recognized how vulnerable he was at this moment.

His life could be in her hands. And he was wise enough to know the truth of it.

He handed the dagger over without question. She quickly cut through the underskirt of her gown first, ripping the fine fabric into strips for bandages. Then she cut across his trews, making the opening wide enough for her to assess the damage. She peered closely at it, taking in the gruel of loose flesh laying in tangles around the main slice, evidence he'd been cut with a dirty blade. "Ye grabbed my satchel?"

"Aye," he said, pointing to the horse. After taking his hand and telling him to hold it on the wound, she stood and moved to the horse, but not before ripping her gown up to the waist, something more practical since she had trews on underneath.

He watched her, the sweat still gathering on his brow, the pain evident with any movement he made or any time she touched him. After taking out her small healer sack, she threw the skirt of her outfit onto the ground, then knelt on it, pulling her poultice out and an odd contraption that she unfolded and snapped into place.

"What is that?"

"Hold it, please. 'Tis something my aunt created to help wash wounds without drenching all the clothing. It guides the water away. Ye will see it soon." She moved his hand aside and pressed really hard against his wound. The heaviest bleeder was the one on the front of his thigh.

He closed his eyes, holding the groan of pain inside.

"Sorry, but the key to yer survival is threefold. We must stop the bleeding, then treat it with this poultice to prevent the fever, then ye must drink as much as ye can."

"Why… drink?" The pace of his words coming out was a strong clue as to the strength of the body, her mother had always said.

His words were a struggle.

"Because Mama always says water is the most

important to put the fever out. 'Tis like putting cold water with hot water to make it warm." She stopped her pressure, then looked at it. "'Tis slowing, but not stopping yet. I must push harder. Forgive me."

He closed his eyes again to stifle his groan after she increased the pressure, and it gave her the opportunity to study him. His strong jawline clenched at the moment, and he had the longest dark eyelashes she'd ever seen on a man. The kind lasses wished for. His skin was bronzed from the sun, and he had a small scar on the side of his face not far from his eye.

He opened his eyes, and they locked gazes. "A favor?" he whispered. "If you are to leave me once you've fixed me, I'll not stop you. But I have a favor first."

She didn't move, so fascinated with the man that she didn't wish to pull back. His closeness did something to her she'd not experienced before. Oh, she'd seen men's bodies from a distance, glances that had sent tingles to her nether region, but this was different.

This came directly from his heat. His being. It was an aura about him that reached out to her. Only to her.

"I'll grant it," she said, surprising herself that she trusted him enough to grant him the favor. She owed him nothing. He owed her.

His hand reached for her cheek, cupping it gently and tugging her forward until their lips met. His lips were still warm, and they melded with hers. She thought to end it, but curiosity got the best of her. She leaned into him and parted her lips just a sliver, and he took advantage, slipping his tongue into her mouth, seeking hers.

Reyna became lost in all that was Wulf. He tasted of apple, the one he must have just eaten, yet he was all man. His movements were gentle, surprisingly appealing, and a stark contrast to the beasts who had assaulted her. When he ended the kiss, he leaned his forehead against hers, his breath heating her insides as if she were near a hearth in winter.

"My thanks to you for sharing your sweetness," he whispered, his breathing irregular. He kissed her forehead and set her away from him. "And many thanks for staying with me, using your skills."

She blushed and leaned back on her heels, taking the cloth from his wound, pleased to see the bleeding had stopped. She covered the wound with her mother's poultice and wrapped his leg with the inside layer of her skirt, though lifting his leg just to get the cloth underneath caused him to take a shuddering breath. So when she had to pull it tight before tying it, he paled and closed his eyes.

"I'm sorry, but I cannae risk it breaking open again. A tight bandage will prevent that." She made sure the part against the wound was clean.

"You learned much from your mother. You are more skilled than the English men who call themselves physicians."

"I had many teachers. My mother and my aunts are all healers, so heed my advice. If ye see it bleeding again, ye must put pressure on it to stop it. It could start up any time."

He nodded, watching her intently. She picked up the skein and put a powder inside. "Here, drink this."

He took it from her, lifted it to his lips for a sip, then asked, "What did you put in it?"

"'Tis a mix to keep the water from making ye worse, and also to help with yer pain a bit."

"Why would water make me worse? It is only water."

"Water can have things inside that can make you sick. My mother boils any water we drink. Said they learned the hard way about things in water. She talks often of a time when they were forced to boil water to keep from dying. They all noticed that the entire clan had less sickness when they boiled the water, so it became a habit at Clan Matheson. But since we cannot boil that water, I need to put in this powder instead. It has been successful thus far."

"I'd ask you to explain yourself, but I'm too tired to listen. May I sleep?" His eyes drooped, and he started to lean, so she stopped him.

"Aye."

She fussed with her belongings, then helped him lie down.

He pointed to the horse. "I'll take the fur under the saddle. My sire always travels with one." When she returned with it, he asked. "Will you be here when I awaken, or do you plan on leaving soon?"

"'Tis dark now, so I will stay the night with ye.

Make sure yer wound doesnae open up again. I dinnae like to ride in the dark alone."

She made her way to the burn and washed the blood from her hands, then refreshed her face. By the time she turned back to him, he was sound asleep.

She sighed, wondering what the hell life would bring her on the morrow.

# CHAPTER TWELVE

WULF AWOKE WITH a start from the pain in his leg. Once he adjusted his leg a bit, it became bearable again. He sighed, scanning the darkness around him, wondering where Reyna was until she reached back to touch the clothing near his wound.

He said, "You can look. I am awake. Though I'm unsure what good touching it does for you."

"I touch to feel if it is soaked with blood. 'Tis no' wet so go back to sleep."

"I doubt I can," he said, reaching for her waist. "We would probably benefit from each other's heat. I am cold, so you are probably frigid."

She scooted back, her bottom not far from his pelvis. He was glad the wound was there so she couldn't tuck in tightly. He'd not be able to withstand that much temptation. "I feared you left me, Reyna. My thanks for staying."

"Not for long. I'm no' going back to York with ye. I'll head north, whether I have to walk or ride a horse."

"You will take my horse. I owe you that much for staying with me. I'm sorry for the situation we find ourselves in. I should not have brought you to York. I should have left you in Berwick." He glanced around, glad to see they hadn't been disturbed by any more marauders. The sound of the burn nearby and the animals were something he rarely paid much attention to, but on this night, he found all the sounds pleasing. Was it because he hadn't known if he would wake up?

A slight breeze carried through the forest, washing her scent over him and carrying with it a strange sense of longing. He had never felt this way before, and it was almost like a pull, drawing him closer to her without him even realizing it.

The ground was damp, but the fur beneath them kept him dry. Even though they were not touching, he was mesmerized by her, completely captivated by her presence. His heart raced as he tried to make sense of the feelings bubbling inside him. Was this love or something else?

He watched her from behind, so close that he could feel the heat of her body and could smell the sweet scent of her skin. He felt his heart swell, and the strange feeling inside him grew stronger.

She rolled onto her back, then to her side to face him. Her words came out in a quiet calm, oddly comforting to him. "Ours is a verra unusual relationship, Wulfstan. I should have walked away since ye stole me away from my group, my clanmates, and my friends. But instead, I dinnae hate ye, so I will no' desert ye until ye are hale. I apparently have a healer's soul, and no matter how I wish to ignore it, I canno'."

She smiled at him shyly, her eyes twinkling in

the moonlight of the night, and he wished to drown in them. He knew then, without a doubt, that this was love. A love that he could feel in every fiber of his being. A love that he had never thought possible, and yet here it was, daring him to ignore it. He surely could not.

"I have no words to speak of your soul other than it is one of the finest I've ever met." His whisper echoed in the still of the night, adding to the ambience of their time together.

She touched her fingers to his lips. "Ye must conserve yer strength. But please tell me why ye hate yer sire so. I would be interested in hearing the truth because it saddens me. I dinnae know what I would do without my sire. I adore him."

"My sire killed my mother."

He waited for her reaction but didn't get much, just a questioning arch in her brow.

"Tell me more, please."

He didn't blame her. It was an unbelievable accusation, especially because the man had never been held accountable for what he did.

"When I was six and ten summers, I came home from visiting with a friend, and I heard my parents arguing. Tryana was with our uncle, so I stopped to listen.

"Understand that my sire was always brutal. He was never kind to my mother, barking orders at her and striking her occasionally. We never knew why. Their arguments were always quiet and private until he would bellow, and my mother would weep silently. Something I never understood."

"The beating or the weeping?"

"The weeping. My mother never made a sound when she cried around my father. She always took his belligerence, nodding and not looking at him, then crying into her linen square after they were done."

"It could be just the way she was."

"I don't believe that. There was more to it than that. The day I crept home alone, I watched him. We lived in a sizable manor home with an upstairs and a balcony. When I arrived, I saw my mother at the top of the staircase, and she shook her head at me, telling me to stay quiet. So I did. Now I regret it, but that's what I did. She was crying, and my father was pacing and yelling. I did what she asked because I wished to find out why he hated her so, so I waited, and then I watched him completely lose his temper. He picked up the heavy iron door stop, hit her on the back of the head, then shoved her down the stairs. I hollered and ran to her as soon as he picked up the door stop, but I was too late. She was already dead. The entire incident only took seconds, less than a minute. How I wish I'd done more, moved faster. Something to prevent his cruelty. Even though I disliked my father at the time, I had no idea he would resort to killing my mother."

"Oh, Wulf. If it happened that quickly, there was naught ye could have done. How awful. I canno' imagine losing my mother, much less watching her fall to her death. What did yer sire say?"

"That she was clumsy and tripped, falling down the stairs. It is exactly what he told the sheriff

when he came. I had to help him bury her, but
we took her far into the field, dug a hole, and
he rolled her into it. I vomited when I saw her.
Vomited and ran away."

"Oh, Wulf."

"He got away with murder. He doesn't know
that I saw the entire incident, but I swore I
would retaliate someday. I have spent my time
trying to earn enough to support my sister and
me so we wouldn't be split up once I killed him,
but perhaps I waited too long. Whoever her
betrothed is, I doubt he is worthy of my sister's
devotion. I'm sure it was the coin that motivated
our sire, nothing else. I must find out and save her
from my father, see what this Gareth Ward is like.
I think it is time for me to repay him for taking
my mother's life, even if I am imprisoned for it."

"Is that what kept ye from doing it before?"

"Aye. If I were imprisoned, there would be no
one to watch over Tryana. I do not trust him at
all. He was always ruthless when it came to me
and not much better to Tryana."

"Is that what ye plan to do while here in York?"

"Aye, as soon as I return to York, I will purchase
another horse and go find my sister. I plan to pay
Gareth Ward a visit, then I'll get her away. He has
the reputation as one who beats his wife, and I'll
not subject her to such a life."

Reyna sighed, leaned over, and kissed him full
on the mouth.

"Ye will need another horse for me. I'm going
with ye as long as ye promise I can return to
Berwick after."

Wulf was dumbfounded. "You have my word. I thank you, lass."

Then he kissed her thoroughly.

# CHAPTER THIRTEEN

REYNA KNEW ANYONE in her clan would tell her that she had surely lost her mind, but none of her clan had kissed Wulfstan de Gray either.

Reyna could not get it out of her head that she had little to no control over her own actions and reactions to the man. How could she not have known that he would kiss her back? Could it be that she wanted him to kiss her as much as she did? The man was practically a stranger, yet he had her coming undone. He was a wolf, and she was a hawk, and it seemed it would be a dangerous union. Was she willing to take the chance?

He was breaking down all the walls she had carefully built over the years, and she found herself allowing the weakening.

Reyna could not explain it, but she knew she had to stay away from him for her own sake. He was dangerous for her and her clan because he was English, and honestly, she was a bit frightened of his power over her.

Whatever the reason and odd hold he had over her, she decided to help him find his sister and get her away from the cruel baron. Once that was done, she'd return to Berwick and her clan.

It sounded as though the only one who would fight for Tryana was Wulf. And after losing their mother the way they had, she couldn't help but wish to help the two siblings.

The two mounted and headed back toward York, surprised to find another horse not far down the road, placidly chewing grass. It looked to be one left by the marauders, and she was pleased to see there were no bodies on the ground.

He said, "I know your thoughts. They all could survive most of their injuries."

She climbed down and mounted the other horse since it was easier for her to move. They moved slower than usual, being ever cognizant of other riders. They did not need any more skirmishes along the way. "My grandsire always said traveling was safer in the morn because the marauders were busy holding their heads from the ale they drank the previous night. I hope it continues this way."

"Amuse me and tell me about your favorite memories of your clan. Having lived in a small home without many relatives, I'm curious to hear what clan life was like."

Reyna thought over many of their memorable times. "One of my favorites was over the summer when the water heated up from the sun. We live on the coast of Beauly Firth and while there are mud flats, swimming is best at this one spot where the bottom is nice and sandy. I used to love it when my sire would run in the water carrying me and flinging me off into the deep water. And I also recall my sire doing the same with my mother. That would send me into fits and giggles, especially when Da would race against my uncles with their wives.

"I think one of the reasons we are so blessed is because the Matheson brothers married cousins—two Ramsays and one Cameron. And because of that, we often traveled to Clan Ramsay or Clan Grant for the summer festival. That was so much fun. We had obstacle courses and foot races, archery challenges, horseback riding. And we had swimming challenges there as well because both had ropes from trees hanging over the lochs. We would run with the rope, swing over the water, and flip or dive into the loch. We looked forward to it each year. Those were the only places I ever traveled to other than Inverness to market or for fabric."

"Is that where you learned to stand on the back of your horse?"

Reyna was surprised he'd caught her in such an event. "Ye watched me more than I knew."

"Aye, you are a beautiful woman, Reyna. Someday you'll believe it and tread more carefully."

She couldn't think of a witty response to that compliment and she knew she blushed. "My thanks." She had to admit that being called beautiful by this man pleased her.

"So who taught you that skill? It cannot be easy."

"My cousin, Lily. Her father taught her. We

have so many tales of battles and fights, but Uncle Quade's is one of my favorites. Someday, you'll hear the story of how he saved his wife by using his bow and arrow while standing on his horse's back. Grandsire still talks about it."

They neared the river at the edge of York so their conversation stopped. "I have no coin for the tolls. Do ye?" she asked.

"Aye, I have plenty. We'll head back to the inn, then find out exactly where Gareth Ward lives. I must speak with my sister. Offer her the chance to back out of the betrothal before it's too late. You know how English law is. Once she is married, she has no rights." He rubbed his leg all the while they rode, something she couldn't ignore. The pain had to be substantial, especially since it was a sizable wound. She couldn't help but think that she didn't have enough poultice to keep him from getting the fever.

Everyone knew how deadly that green liquid could be. Perhaps they would need to find a healer.

Reyna hated that ignorant belief that women were inferior. "Sad but true. Did ye know that I have an aunt who is chieftain of her clan? My family believes women have value and I was raised that way. 'Tis verra hard for me to adjust to the English way."

Once they returned to the inn, she'd cleaned and bandaged his wound properly, giving him another touch of the potion for pain, though she had little left. Then she insisted he rest a bit. It had been a long cold night in the woods and though the journey back to the inn was short, it left them both exhausted. She'd searched for Emmot upon their return, but he was nowhere to be seen. Wulf had told her to let Emmot go, that he was probably out searching for them.

It was early in the afternoon before they headed out toward the baron's estate. "Wulf, dinnae be foolish and think ye can do anything where ye will need to run to safety. Running is no' for ye at present."

"I am aware of that, dear lady. My thanks for worrying about me." They stopped their horses to chat at the crossroad to the baron's castle. "This is the path we take to the castle. I can see the turrets up ahead. I pray they'll let me speak with my sister."

Reyna snorted and then giggled.

"Did you just snort?"

"I did." She laughed at him, and he smiled, something she rarely saw.

"Why?"

"Because ye are English, and ye think so differently than the Scots."

"What would you have me do? Since you are so experienced at subterfuge, I'll hear your suggestion."

"Ye jest, but my grandparents were spies, so I've been raised to think differently. Ye must think of the opposite."

"What?" he asked, turning his horse to face her. "How could we possibly do anything else?"

She rolled her eyes, the movement reminding her of her dear cousin Isla who rolled her eyes frequently. "I would search for the secret passageway."

"What passageway? How would you know that one exists?"

"Any castle built in Scotland has a secret exit. Usually, a hidden doorway in the main bedroom, sometimes to the bairn's bedchambers. And it leads to a door on the other side of the curtain wall hidden in the surrounding forest. Just some way to escape if attacked. The only way the chieftain and his family could get away."

"But that doorway cannot be easy to find."

"Nay, but it could be done. If we find it, we could get inside and out without the baron ever knowing. We could sneak Tryana out."

He paused and glanced about them. No one was nearby. "How do you presume to find this entrance if it's hidden in the woods?"

"Slowly and carefully. Follow me. I have an idea."

He motioned for her to take the lead, something that surprised her. Wulf didn't take orders from many. She set her horse to a nice canter and took a third path she'd noticed in the woods a bit ahead, one that was definitely a path, but not well traveled.

That usually meant it went nowhere. "Since this is no' a regular path, my guess was the baron had his men check the doorway, make sure it was clear at least every other moon. Summer's growth could make it difficult to find if not tended occasionally."

They set off down the path that wove its way

through the forest, enough light filtering through the trees to show the way. She kept her gaze on the ground, occasionally glancing around to make sure they weren't being followed. She'd been right. The path did lead nowhere.

"Here," she said, tugging on her reins and stopping.

"What are you seeing that I'm not seeing? All I see are bushes." Wulf motioned to the overgrown trees on either side. "There is absolutely nothing here. This path leads to naught."

"Aye," she agreed, giving him a saucy look because she knew she'd been correct. "But look back." She pointed to the path they'd just taken. "If you stand at the end of the path and look back, you'll be able to see the indentation in the foliage we are looking for." She could see the doubt in his eyes, but she thought it best to let him discover the doorway, so she pointed in the direction she would have gone. "The shadows hide it. 'Tis brilliantly placed."

He turned his horse and took a moment to study the path, then he led his horse back and forth, then back and forth again, until he found the spot. "Clever lass." He dismounted with a wince after he shot a shocked look at her. "Allow me to check to see if it opens."

"It will. I am sure of it. There were no keys made for these hidden passages."

He rubbed his leg, a delayed cringe from the pain of landing, something she was glad to see. The pain was getting to be more tolerable for him. And after the brief beating she'd taken from the bastards who'd yanked her off her horse, she was glad her own bruises were feeling better. Her bruises didn't show, but she was reminded about them whenever she turned a certain way. And jumping off a horse was sure to pain them both. She did carry a bit of guilt over his wound.

If not for her attempt to escape, he would not have been injured. And she shuddered every time she thought about what would have happened to her if he hadn't come along and given her the bow and arrow.

She knew the truth. It was his fault she'd been in such a position, but she still wished him a speedy recovery. He took slow, careful steps over to the door, tugging on it lightly before using both hands to pull. The door opened wide on the second yank. "'Tis too dark to see."

"I'm going with ye. There will be a light source. If not, they cut holes into the ground above for light or set stones just so. Ye will see. Leave the door open. No one will be along to see it."

She propped the door with a rock and stepped in ahead of him, but he grabbed her waist. "I will go first, not you, lass." He kissed her neck as he stepped around her. "I do have some honor."

Her neck tingled where his lips had touched her sensitive skin. What was happening to her? This English man was making her daft.

No matter. They would get Wulf's sister away this night, and she could be homeward-bound on the morrow.

He limped along the narrow passageway, finding his way easily because she'd been right about the light above. Every so often, a shaft of light cut through the ceiling, guiding their progress. His hand went up overhead several times to knock the cobwebs aside, and that small movement made her grateful he'd gone first.

Reyna could hear the plodding of his feet ahead of her, his every movement echoing in the tunnel. The sound was a comfort to her. He wouldn't leave her unless he had a reason to believe it was necessary.

And suddenly, she remembered. The feeling was there, the sensation of being held down, the attacker's weight making her feel like she couldn't breathe, and the anger and confusion. She could hear it all. And then the silence.

She felt a tear slip down her cheek and brushed it away, angry with herself for letting the memories get to her again. She had a job to do, and if she were to cease being a Ramsay guard, then she could head home on the morrow. Make a stop at Berwick, then on to Clan Ramsay, then home to Black Isle and Clan Matheson. Just as Isla had done. She'd hoped to go home in love, bringing along a nice Scottish guard who traveled with King Robert enchanted by her personality and abilities as an archer, but it hadn't happened. It was time to give up on her dream. Let go of her feelings of failure. She didn't want those feelings to rapidly slip past her, dragged along by the tide, because she'd never taken the time to deal with them.

His voice interrupted her thought. "There, up ahead. I believe I see a set of steps." He stopped and turned to her, his hand going straight to his thigh.

"I can go up if ye think ye canno'."

"Nay. I must go. Tryana does not know you, so she would scream if you entered her chamber. I have to go. I'll get through the pain. Do not concern yourself."

"Fine. I'll let ye go up. I will follow if ye dinnae return within a few moments."

"Agreed."

# CHAPTER FOURTEEN

WULF IGNORED THE pain as he climbed up the staircase, surprisingly not very steep, but still a challenge. When he reached the top, there was a landing and railing to hang on to, something he thought was wonderfully created.

Reyna touched his shoulder. "Listen first. This could be the baron's private bedchamber."

He nodded, knowing she was correct.

All was quiet inside, so he reached for the door handle and moved it slightly inward, hoping to get a glimpse of what chamber they were in. A shaft of light came through, enough to light up Reyna's beautiful face when he glanced over his shoulder. At this odd time, he had the sudden urge to stop and stare at her beauty.

But he didn't, instead peeking inside the door. It was a small chamber, one probably attached to a main bedchamber. And there stood his beautiful sister, tears covering her cheeks, wearing a wrinkled gown, one that looked as though she'd been digging a ditch in it. And there were shadows toward the bottom.

"Wulf?" His sister moved hesitantly toward him. "Is that you?"

"Tryana," he whispered, holding his finger to his lips. "I'm here to take you away. And what were you doing? Your knees are bloodied."

"Hush," she whispered. "I was doing penance for my errors. I have to kneel in front of the cross until he returns. He will be back shortly. You must go. He'll whip you. And what is wrong with your leg?" She sounded stronger than he recalled, but he was glad of it. The bastard hadn't beaten her down yet.

He didn't wish to know the truth of how his dear sister knew that the baron would whip him if caught. "My leg will be fine, so do not concern yourself. Come with me. I'm here to take you away." He stepped into the chamber, and Reyna came in behind him.

"Who is she?" She peered over his shoulder warily.

"A friend. Someone I trust. Now grab whatever you need, and I'll get you away." He spoke in a tone low enough not to be heard by anyone else, but one that let her know he was growing impatient. They could not get caught. He gestured toward the other chamber. "Go ahead, but hurry."

"Nay, not now. Come back in the middle of the night. When he's not around with all his friends to do his horrible tasks. I do not wish to risk getting caught because the punishment would be more than I could bear. We must be careful about this. He's coming. Go." She glanced over her shoulder and when she turned back, she shook her head. "Go!"

"Come with me."

"Not now. Hurry!" She pushed him toward the door. "I'll explain later. Come back."

"Midnight. I'll be here at midnight."

He closed the door just in time to hear the other door open. "Why are you up? You have not been excused from your penance yet. What were you doing?" The voice was not one he recognized, but he was familiar with the tone. An old man who thought to order his dear sister around, control her every movement. He had to do something, but he knew he was in no shape to fight with another man at the moment. And he had no weapon with him.

"I needed the chamber pot. Please excuse me."

"Do what you must and return to your penance. I will wait right here."

Reyna tugged on him, so he followed her back down the staircase. She had no idea how difficult it was to turn his back on his sister, but he also knew he was in no position to fight. If he stepped back into that chamber, they would all be prisoners. He had to use his head, something he rarely did, instead allowing his emotions to drive him. If he had any at all.

They headed down the passageway, the echo of the boots telling them they were not followed. Yet.

Once they reached the end and opened the door, Wulf stepped out and found the nearest tree to lean against because he was exhausted. It was nearing the supper hour, so they did not have much time, but at his current pace, would he make it back? What was wrong with him? He'd never been this weak from a short jaunt.

"Healing will drain your strength," Reyna said as she closed the door behind her, scanning the area for any unwanted guests.

"All right. That explains why I cannot move, but can you explain why my sister refused to leave when she was clearly being abused by her betrothed? Her knees had bloodied her gown. What else has the bastard done to her?" His hands were flexed at his hips as he gained the ability to breathe back, huffing and puffing from their small task.

She moved over to stand in front of him. "You mean the evil committed by the baron besides fixing her brain to believe the wrong thing? Some people do that. 'Tis trickery at its worst. Making ye believe that everything is yer fault when it clearly is no'."

"I've heard of that, but it doesn't explain why she refused to leave."

"She is worried about ye, feared ye would be caught. She is correct in that assessment. If she had come with us, the baron would have discovered her missing immediately and followed us out the door and down the passageway. Ye are a tad bit slow at the moment. I think she was protecting ye. She's right. 'Twill be much safer at midnight, and that will give her a chance to pack her things. Mayhap there is something she did not wish to leave behind."

"My mother's necklace. She was not wearing it. Perhaps you are correct." He pushed himself up from the tree and cupped her cheek. "Where did you gain all that wisdom, my lady?" He stepped closer, inhaling her flowery scent, seeing the fine tremor in her hands when he closed the distance between them.

He had thought of this moment ever since their first kiss last eve, and yet when it finally happened, it was more beautiful than he had ever imagined. His beloved Reyna, the woman he hadn't known he'd been searching for—whom he had finally found—was standing in front of him now, her eyes full of love and devotion, her lips trembling in anticipation.

And so he kissed her. His kiss was gentle yet passionate as if it encompassed many lifetimes of love and longing. Her lips melded with his, and he was lost in all that was Reyna: her warmth, her strength, her beauty. Wulf held her close and felt the beat of her heart, and in that moment he knew with absolute certainty that he would never be able to let her go.

What was happening to him? His very being was overtaken by this siren, this woman who was the only person able to distract him from his purpose. He ended the kiss and held his hand out to her. "Come, we must get back before I fall down. Since we are to return at midnight, I need to rest."

Once they mounted their horses, they headed back down the path, letting their horses set the pace. There was no hurry. "'Tis a lovely day. No mist or rain," he said.

"Ye should travel deep into the Highlands to see true beauty. The mountains, the deep forests full of wildlife and wildflowers. Ye can get lost in the Highland enchantment. We have a faerie waterfall not far from us, one of my favorite places to be. 'Tis so calm and peaceful, the birdsong mesmerizing in the summer." She glanced over at him and smiled.

His foolish heart skipped a beat at the change in her. The look of sweet contentment on her face presently was much more pleasing than the fury and the sparks he'd seen since he abducted the lass. He changed the subject quickly, not willing to talk about where he'd traveled in the past. "Question for you, lass. Have you ever been in love before?"

"Nay, have ye?"

He shook his head. "I was hoping you would say you had. I've often wondered what it would feel like. Wondered if I would recognize it when it fell upon me, though I can only envision how it would happen. I never thought about it before, but you make my mind wander to odd places."

She blushed, something he could see easily. "I think 'tis a fine compliment ye just gave me, so I'll say many thanks to ye." She glanced down at her hands and sighed, a sound he hadn't heard from her yet. "Since I'm the chieftain's daughter, I've not had anyone try to court me. They look, come closer, then run in the opposite direction. And when I've visited Ramsay land, I'm related to almost all of the unmarried men there. We dinnae travel much."

"Truly? I'm surprised. And your father hasn't mentioned betrothing you to anyone?"

"Nay, my mother believes in letting her daughters choose their own husband. I've had many cousins who love to talk about how wonderful love is. Isla and I asked Aunt Merewen and Aunt Sorcha when we would know who to choose."

"And their answer?"

"It surprised me." She turned her head in an attempt to readjust the loose hairs that had escaped her plait, the breeze quite lovely in the morn. "They said love will find ye when ye least expect it."

He didn't try to hide his surprise at that comment. Had he known anyone who believed in such an odd custom? Allowing the women to choose their own husband whenever they were ready was something unusual. His father hadn't waited long to make a betrothal for Tryana, one he surely profited from. That brought him back to his present problem. He couldn't help but wonder where he would take Tryana once she escaped.

"Where will ye take Tryana?"

Amazed that she'd followed his train of thought, he shrugged his shoulders. "I'm not sure. Probably to my aunt and uncle who live in the Borderlands."

"Ye trust them?"

"I do. But I'm not sure I can trust the baron

not to chase her. I once told her if she ever found herself in trouble and I wasn't around to help her that she could go to an abbey. Any abbey will do. She's of age to make her own decisions." He had to make a decision as to what would be best for her if they managed to get her away at midnight. He couldn't take her back to the inn where her father stayed. He would break the door down and take her back.

He needed to focus, stop allowing the dark-haired beauty to distract him.

Before Reyna, all he'd focused on was the day he'd finally be able to drive his sword through his sire's black heart, but now he had other desires. Like maybe having a little doe with Reyna. One who looked just like her.

Or keeping her safe while he hunted his sire.

Or perhaps staying in Berwick for a while and then traveling to Scotland with her.

For her, he'd put his sword-wielding days in the past if she asked him, once he saved Tryana and made his father pay for his sins. He could envision a life better than he'd ever thought he deserved.

But the happiness wasn't fully realized.

Not until he made sure his sire couldn't hurt her his sister or Reyna.

<hr/>

They made it back to the inn without consequence. Reyna helped him down from his horse, then they moved inside. He stopped at the desk and said, "Send two platters of whatever your supper meal is within the hour. And whatever fruit pastry you have."

The innkeeper nodded, "Aye, right away, my lord."

They were about to move above stairs when a sheriff opened the door to the inn, stopping when his gaze fell upon Wulf.

"Wulfstan de Gray?"

"Aye," he answered, as curious about the man's identity as she was if she could guess by the confused expression on his face.

"I'll speak with you outside."

Wulf followed him out, and she trailed behind him to see what exactly was happening. This was her opportunity to tell a sheriff she was being held captive, but she would not. Everything had changed between them.

Everything.

Once they were both outside, two men approached him from opposite sides while the sheriff spoke. "Wulfstan de Gray, you are under arrest for being a traitor to our King Edward. Put your hands behind your back."

"What? What did I do?"

"Have you not deserted the garrison assigned to you? Were you not to return within two days?"

"Aye, but I've been detained." He pushed the first man away, but then two more came closer to enforce the sheriff's orders.

"Let it be known that we found you in an inn in the presence of this lass. We arrest you for treason to our mighty King Edward of England."

Emmot came around the corner leading his horse. "I will follow, Captain."

She was so glad to see Emmot, something that surprised her. He must have been searching for them and returned to the inn when he'd failed to locate them. Perhaps he could help with this situation because she was at a loss as to how to help Wulf.

Reyna tried to say something but Wulf looked back over his shoulder at her after they forced him onto a horse. "Reyna, find my sister. Please do as we promised. Do not worry about me."

"Where are you taking him?" Frantic, she looked from one sheriff to another, but their expressions told her they were not interested in telling her anything at all.

"To a prison north of London. He will see the justice of the peace in a sennight or two."

"Two sennights?"

"Reyna, I'm counting on you. Please go after her. You are my only hope. Please."

She could do little else but watch in vain as ten men surrounded the man she'd fallen in love with, now tied as any common criminal would be.

Headed toward London.

They were still within her line of sight when another group approached her, people she barely noticed until they stood directly in front of her.

"Reyna? Are ye hale?" a male voice called out to her.

"Maitland? Is it truly ye? I'm so glad to see ye. Please help me. They have arrested Wulfstan, and we must get him out." Maitland Menzie was the man in charge of their mission, the man she'd hoped would have found her long ago. She was so glad to see him that she wished to hug him, though she was unsure if he would receive it well.

He stood in front of her, his hands on his hips. "Reyna, I see ye've been struck in the face. Ye have shadowed bags under yer eyes and ye are about to fall apart. I think mayhap ye should take a seat under that tree and explain all to me. The sheriffs have the man I would suspect as the guilty party but ye are ready to defend him? We must chat." He pointed to a tree across the street away from the inn while the sheriffs headed down the street with their prisoner well-guarded.

She nodded, staring after Wulf's disappearing frame, pleased to see Emmot behind him. When they were out of eyesight, she moved toward the tree, the sudden realization as to how ridiculous her explanation sounded to Maitland since she'd been taken captive by the man. Her cousins came with him, along with a Matheson guard she knew well. Would they accept her story? She wouldn't blame them if they didn't believe her because even she was aware that she sounded daft at the moment.

"Maitland, I will explain all. Cadyn, Ysenda, please listen to me though I sound daft. Ye are my cousins and know me well enough. Will ye hear my story? Please? Lewis? Give me a few moments to explain."

Now she was trying to save the very same man who had kidnapped her. Maitland followed her across the street, Cadyn, Ysenda, and Lewis behind him. Tears misted her gaze as she was so glad to see someone she truly trusted. Once they were away from prying ears, she threw her arms around Maitland's shoulders and buried her face into his chest, sobbing quietly.

"Ye are comfortable in this inn? Wulf did not mistreat ye?" he asked while she clung to him. "He is no' the one who put the shadows on yer cheek?"

She stepped back for a moment, understanding how odd her request must sound to the leader of the Scottish patrol. "Aye, this inn is a safe place and he did kidnap me, but we came to an understanding. He didnae hurt me, and I was returning to Berwick on the morrow. But now I need yer help. I'm so glad to see all of ye." Her voice dropped to a whisper and she leaned toward the group in front of her. "I'm no' overly fond of England."

Maitland crossed his arms and said, "I cannae help free him of whatever crime he has committed. This is England and I dinnae know the man at all."

"I understand, but I need yer help to free his sister. She's being held by a cruel baron. Please help me."

"I'll need to hear more before I agree to help ye. For now, we'll get settled so I can hear all that has transpired. Then I'll make my decision as to whether we return with or without ye, Reyna. I'm here to help, but I still must consider our main mission."

"Many thanks to ye, Maitland." She swiped at her tears and had a sudden understanding as to why Maitland was chosen by her grandsire. He was a level-headed, trustworthy man who would listen to her before coming to his decision. That was all she could ask in this odd situation she found herself in.

He motioned to two of his companions. "Lewis and Ysenda, please take the horses to the town stable. See that they are fed and brushed. Then join us in the inn for the evening meal. We'll spend the night here. I'm assuming ye have a chamber or two?"

"Aye, he has paid for two already and he had just ordered supper. Come in. I need to think." Exhausted by all she'd been through, this new development was difficult to sort through in her mind. But she thought it best to get the worst over in the beginning.

"Maitland, I'm in love with Wulf. We cannae let him die."

## CHAPTER FIFTEEN

REYNA WAS SO upset she had a hard time thinking clearly, but she was also grateful that Maitland had arrived to help her through this travesty now called her life.

She had been kidnapped, brought to York against her will, escaped, been attacked by a group of marauders, saved by her kidnapper, fallen in love with the man, and watched him taken to prison. She promised to save his sister from the evil baron, and then she would do what she could to save him.

What had happened to her?

She explained to Maitland all that had happened, then looked at him and said, "Please help me, Maitland."

"Of course I will," he said, frowning. "I must admit, this is not the manner in which I envisioned this meeting going as I expected to be fighting de Gray. But ye arenae the first to fall for your kidnapper. I know what is happening here, Reyna. I know how ye are feeling. Ye arenae to blame for any of this, which is why I am here."

"Many thanks for agreeing to help me," she

replied, swiping at the remaining tears. "I dinnae know what to do. I dinnae want to appear disloyal, but I wish to help Wulf and his sister."

"Of course ye do," he said kindly. "In time everything will come to pass, and we will get through this, but ye look exhausted, and if we are to be ready at midnight, we all must eat. Ye look as if ye've just been in a fight too. But I'll give ye time to think on everything, see if you've neglected any part of yer tale while we eat."

He strode over to the innkeeper and ordered their food for their table instead of above stairs as had been previously ordered. When he returned to sit, before he sat down, he looked at Cadyn and said, "Aye, I ordered double for ye. Double lamb stew with extra carrots, the largest loaf of bread they have, and a platter full of fruits and pastries. We will wait for the ale."

Cadyn leaned back and smiled, the time when he looked most like his grandfather. He had the good looks of his mother, but he often tried to look gruff like his father and grandfather, but it just didn't work yet.

"This eve, we focus on getting Tryana free. Ye know where she is and how to find the passageway? Can ye find it in the dark?" Maitland grabbed a goblet of ale from a sideboard, offering her one.

"Aye, I marked the place with a set of branches, just like Grandmama taught me." She glanced around, the fear of seeing Wulf's sire something she couldn't get out of her mind, but they were the only ones in the dining hall because it was a bit late.

"Dinnae worry about an old man. I'll take care of him if he tries to interfere. Now the main issue is what to do with her once we save her. We cannae bring her back here."

"I see the wisdom of that. He would force her to return as soon as he saw her. And he will look for Wulf or me once he learns she's missing, so she cannae remain with us."

"My suggestion is to get her out first, then we'll worry about freeing Wulf. And we will."

She couldn't stop the smile from blossoming across her face. "Ye think we can?"

"We will. Ye think I would leave him to the bloody bastards who made the rivers run red from Scottish blood in Berwick? I will get him out if ye wish it, though it may take a little longer. But we will have to hide his sister somewhere safe while we focus on Wulf. I'll remind ye we arenae in Scotland. We dinnae have many allies here."

Maitland was right. She hadn't thought of that. She hadn't thought ahead much at all. So much had happened in such a short time.

"May I make a suggestion?" Cadyn asked, folding his hands on the table in front of him.

"Please do," Maitland said, giving him his full attention.

Reyna nodded, looking for any suggestions at the moment, even bad ones.

Cadyn suggested, "I'll escort her to the nearest

abbey. No one can remove her from an abbey without her permission."

Maitland smiled and patted Cadyn's shoulder. "Great idea, lad."

Reyna wanted to jump for joy, but she couldn't believe it would be that simple. "Truly? Her sire cannae remove her?"

"How old is she?" Maitland asked Reyna.

"I think she is nine and ten."

"Then, if she chooses to stay, she can. We would need to pose the question to her before we escort her. She could have an aunt or cousin somewhere. But it could prove to be the safest place for her while we go for Wulf."

The conversation stopped as the food and drinks were placed on the table. Ysenda and Lewis entered, bickering over something as they joined them, Ysenda with a scowl and Lewis with a grin.

"What happened?" Maitland asked.

"Naught," Lewis was quick to reply.

"Naught. To him, 'twas naught. I said I'd brush the horses down…"

"After I said I would."

"Nay, I did. And ye took the brush out of my hand."

Reyna and Maitland watched the banter bounce back and forth while Cadyn dove into the food as if he'd never eaten before.

"And then he knocked into me, and I fell…"

"Accidentally! I knocked into ye by accident," Lewis chuckled. "Right into the horse droppings."

"I did no'. I was near them, but I missed them." She gave his arm a slight swipe.

"But ye cannae deny the aroma coming from ye." He leaned toward her and sniffed, wrinkling his nose.

Cadyn chortled into his food but said nothing.

Maitland said, "Lewis, enough. Ysenda, he is goading ye. Ye dinnae carry an odor. Now ye both need to sit and eat. We have a serious mission, and I'll no' have any mistakes. Understood?"

Reyna knew that whenever a battle was involved, Maitland brooked no arguing, no fighting, no questioning the leader's decisions. And everyone respected it because he'd seen the worst of it. One bad decision had cost him his wife.

It was probably why Grandsire had chosen Maitland for this mission because no one dared to argue with him when it came to patrol or battle. Outside of battle, he was as even-tempered as anyone could be.

She would never dare to question him. And he was the best thing that could have happened to her. He was going to help her save Tryana.

With Maitland by her side, they'd be successful.

If she could only focus on that and rid her mind of her greatest fear.

That she would never see Wulf again because they would hang him for treason before anyone could free him.

Two hours later, the five took the path less traveled, and Reyna took the lead, looking for the branches she'd left, indicating the door to the passageway was close. The moon was nearly full, giving them enough light to find their way through the area, especially because there were not many trees along the route. There was a thick line of trees between this path and the main one, so they could not be discovered by anyone on the main path, something they all appreciated.

"Are ye sure about the branches?" Maitland asked, scanning the area with his gaze.

"Aye, Grandmama made us do it several times. Ysenda was with me then."

"She did. 'Tis hard to forget Grandmama's teachings," Ysenda added, then pointed. "There. I recognize them."

"Aye! This is exactly where I placed them." She dismounted and led the horse to a nearby tree, where she hooked the reins on a branch. "The door is in that small copse."

Maitland dismounted and turned to the others. "Ye will all stay here and watch the horses. I will go with Reyna. How long is the path, Reyna?"

She shrugged her shoulders, then said, "A quarter the hour mayhap? No more."

"Cadyn, if we dinnae return in half the hour, ye and Ysenda will follow while Lewis waits here. Understood?" Maitland looked from one nodding face to the next.

Maitland tugged on the old wooden door and stepped inside. "There is light most of the way?"

"Aye, during the day. I think 'tis enough moonlight," Reyna replied. "A staircase and a landing at the end. The door goes to Tryana's bedchamber."

"Off we go," he said and stepped into the darkness. Reyna grabbed the back of his tunic, glad to let him go first through the cobwebs. It was pitch black down there. She held her breath as she started after him, wondering how he could see in this thick blackness.

The smell of things she didn't wish to identify assaulted her nostrils as they walked through the dirt path, so she covered her nose with her tunic, the path mostly straight but for two corners lit up by a perfectly placed hole in the ceiling of the tunnel, a lovely moonbeam visible at one spot. Wondering how the aromas could appear stronger now than before, she had to admit that since she had taken a quick nap, her senses were much better now. Glancing over her head at the dirt ceiling and other things hanging down, she couldn't help but wonder if these passages ever caved in. Forcing herself to focus, they continued until they came to the roughly-hewn stone stairs, the light from a few small openings illuminating the steps.

"I see it ahead," she called to him. It was the same landing with a wall on their left and the door directly in front. "We can both fit."

Her eyes had finally adjusted to the darkness making the steps visible. "Can ye see, Maitland? If no', I can go first."

"I can see fine," he whispered, holding his finger to his lips. They climbed the crooked staircase, stopping at the landing outside the door. "Are ye ready?"

"Aye."

He turned the handle and pushed the door open enough to peek inside at the small antechamber with no windows in front of him. Maitland looked around, then stuck his head inside. A small fire blazed in the hearth, but the room was empty. He stepped in, and Reyna came in behind him, both searching for any sign of Tryana. Another door sat in front of them, so he moved forward.

"Wait here," he said. "I will go in."

"Nay!" Reyna said quickly. "I dinnae wish to be caught here alone. 'Tis another door behind me, one I didnae see before."

"Agreed." He turned the handle slowly and opened the door. Reyna felt her heartbeat quicken as it had the last time she and Wulf had come this way. Her breathing became shallow and caught in her throat, fear of meeting the cruel baron and Tryana's sire reaching deep into her belly.

A female voice whispered, "Wulf?"

Reyna stepped to the side of Maitland so Tryana could see her face. "Wulf begged me to come and get ye, bring ye out of here at midnight. I was here with him before. My name is Reyna."

Tryana grabbed a small satchel from a chair and said, "Please take me to my brother."

Maitland closed the door quietly behind Tryana and said, "Reyna, go. Lead the way, and I will bring up the rear."

Reyna didn't wait for any further instructions, so she took Tryana's empty hand and led her back down the passageway, moving as quickly and quietly as possible. Once they reached the end, she moved the door just a touch before Cadyn opened it wide.

"Ye are safe. Did ye find her?" he asked.

Tryana stepped out behind Reyna and nearly walked into Cadyn, who abruptly froze, staring at her.

"Excuse me, if you please," Tryana whispered, peeking at Cadyn before stepping back.

"Yer pardon. 'Tis my fault, my lady." Cadyn hadn't torn his gaze from Tryana yet, something quite unusual for him.

"Tryana, this is my cousin, Cadyn MacAdam, behind ye is Maitland and another cousin, Ysenda Ramsay. And Lewis is a Matheson guard."

"Where is my brother? My father said he was arrested for treason. Is this true? He said they will hang him for sure. Please tell me we can stop that from happening. Or was he lying? My own sire likes to get me agitated with lies." Tryana kneaded her hands with worry, looking from one face to the face. "Is it true?"

Maitland took her bag and placed it on the back of the saddle on his horse. "'Tis true that he was taken, but I plan to go there on the morrow and see if we can free him."

"You can do that?" she asked, clearly surprised at his declaration.

"I will do my best, my lady. But my first concern is yer safety. I fear yer sire and the baron will both come looking for ye. We need a place to hide ye until Wulfstan is free. Do ye have a cousin, anyone ye know in York? A safe place until we set Wulf free?"

"Nay, but my brother always told me that if anything happened, I should go to the nearest abbey and await his arrival. That if our father tried to remove me from there, I could refuse him now that I am nine and ten."

"Then we shall do that. I will have ye ride with Cadyn. We will escort ye there. Ysenda, Lewis, and Cadyn will guard ye at the abbey while Reyna and I go after yer brother. We should return to the abbey with him by the next eve or two days, no more. Be patient, as it may require a bit of trickery. And we are no' exactly sure where they are holding him. It could be London or a closer holding cell."

"I will agree to this. And then where?"

"Back to Scotland if Wulf agrees." Maitland helped her onto the front of Cadyn's horse.

Reyna was pleased to see that Tryana had worn a heavy mantle because the nights could be very cool, especially on horseback.

"Wulf will agree," Tryana replied. "Godspeed with all of us."

"Are ye sure of that?" Reyna asked, unsure of Wulf's willingness to return to Scotland, though it would be the safest place for him, so it made sense.

Did she know her brother had the reputation of being the cruelest captain in the English garrison?

"Aye. Scotland is his favorite place. 'Tis where we were born."

Reyna nearly fell off her horse. What else didn't she know about Wulfstan de Gray?

## CHAPTER SIXTEEN

—⁓—

WULF LEANED BACK against the cold stone wall of the cell he'd been locked in. How long was he going to be in here? The truth would come out eventually.

Everything. Reyna would know the truth. His truth. He prayed he would have the opportunity to explain everything to her before she judged him.

He nearly snorted in the darkness. Prayed. When had he prayed about anything? Ever since he watched his mother die at the hands of his father, he'd lost faith in God. He'd had conversations with nuns and priests since then, but no conversation had ever made sense of his life.

Would he and Tryana ever find a life that didn't have their cruel sire in it?

But until then, he had to pray that Reyna was able to rescue Tryana, get her away from that bastard, Gareth Ward. The bloody bastard would beat her until there was nothing left of her soul. Of that much, he was certain. And after she gave him two sons, he'd probably get rid of her for good.

He had to prevent that from happening.

Wulf had fought hard enough that they'd needed four guards to get him into the cell in the dungeon, even with his wounded leg. Rubbing it, he'd left the bandage in place, not because it would heal better but because Reyna had placed it there so carefully. It served as a reminder of the sweet lass whose kisses were more pleasing than any he'd ever tasted. She'd dressed it with care and then wrapped it with pieces of her gown. He had to love her for that alone.

Did Reyna have any inkling how his feelings for her had grown, just being around her? He'd learned much about her skills and her beauty, but it was the inner makings of Reyna Matheson that fascinated him.

The woman who stayed with him after he was wounded. She stayed with her abductor to make sure he was hale before she planned to leave alone. The woman who could stand up to any man without cowering. Who believed in herself because she knew of her true worth thanks to two loving parents.

This strong woman could have easily escaped, but instead, she'd chosen to stay and help him. She had more moral constitution in the nail on her wee finger than he had in his entire body. A small hope of something more with this woman blossomed inside him, but after she learned the truth about him, he doubted she would have anything to do with him. And since he had abducted and dragged her halfway through England, he wouldn't blame her for never coming near him again.

He heard a sound at the end of the passageway, one the rest of the men in holding cells wouldn't notice because they were all asleep. He was wide awake as if the sun had just risen. The footfalls were soft and deliberate, so he stood, moving toward the door, enough so it could be opened. He had to see who was in the passageway. He kept his gaze locked on the small window in the door where he could see who had passed by.

The boot steps ended at his door. A scraping sounded near the lock, and the door opened. Two men stood before him, one holding the key that had unlocked the cell.

"Time to go, but we will tread carefully past the guard at the top of the stairs. I knocked him out, but he could regain consciousness any time," said the taller man as he pushed Wulf ahead of him, not giving him any time to ponder the present situation.

Wulf nodded, knowing this wasn't the time to express his undying gratitude to be out of prison.

Of course, they weren't out yet.

The man in the lead hung the key on the nail, then strode down the passageway as quietly as a ghost. Wulf's gaze went from side to side as they moved along while the man behind him reached forward to hand him a dagger. Wulf took it and attached the sheath to his belt, grateful for any weapon to be in his hand again.

They climbed the dark staircase, the scratching

sounds of tiny feet carried away from them. Wulf didn't wish to know what could have been in his cell with him. Instead, they moved swiftly to the top of the stairs to a door a horse length away. Another man stood outside the door waiting for them and led them to a door in the back of the curtain wall. A wall taller than any he'd ever seen, one nearly impossible to be scaled, but their escort used a key to unlock the door in the wall and allowed them out. He had no idea what prison he was in or what town. No one had told him anything as they traveled in the night.

Three horses sat outside the gate, and the trio mounted and took off, not yet daring to speak until they were further from the prison walls.

Somehow they'd arranged this escape, leading him to believe the two men with him were two mighty powerful men. He didn't care why. He just was thrilled to be on his way out of that dark, damp prison and back to York.

He didn't ask any questions but took a deep breath of freedom and smiled as they sent the three horses into a fast gallop across the countryside. They were coming from a prison far north of London, but it was nearly daybreak, so they had to move quickly before the sun was up and his absence would be noticed.

Then he prayed he'd find Tryana and Reyna safe and together.

Prayed. Perhaps he should have some faith again. It was worth a try, and he had plenty of time to say his prayers on their way back to York. He needed all the help he could get.

He was on the run until he crossed the border into Scotland.

Home again.

Reyna paced above stairs in their chamber in the inn. She'd wished to go along with Maitland, but he refused, said he was meeting a man who would get Wulf out. Instead, she was forced to pace a chamber, munch on berries, and count as high as she could—over and over again.

Footsteps on the staircase stopped her from moving. She had to wait to see who it was. She'd already be running if she knew it was Wulf, but she didn't know, so she waited, glancing over to make sure the lock was secure on the door.

It was.

Holding her breath, she was disappointed as soon as the door across the corridor opened. Wulf's sire, Wrath. She thought it an oddly appropriate name.

She put her ear to the door to listen to any conversation between the two sets of footsteps she heard. "Go downstairs to lead Wulf up to this chamber once he arrives."

Wulf? Had she heard correctly? He was on his way back here? And his father knew of it?

She opened the door and found herself staring into Wrath de Gray's smiling face. "Wulf is on his way here?"

"Nay, you foolish, gullible lass. But now I can tie you up and throw you on my horse."

He grabbed her hands, but she wouldn't give

up easily. It was this old man against her, and he was a cold-hearted bastard. She knocked her head against his as hard as she could, which proved enough for him to fall back and curse her.

"You wee bitch," he bellowed, and another man raced back up the stairs. "Tie her up and throw her on my horse."

He reached for her, but she could get a fist to his eye before he grabbed her, Wrath grabbing her from behind. She managed to kick the stranger in his bollocks, and he bellowed in pain.

Wrath had her in a bear hug while a third man came out of his chamber, tying up her hands. He reached for her legs, but she put a boot heel into one's face and her other foot into a shoulder with a hard kick.

"Get her. Do ye two weaklings think ye can control a wee lass? Is she too much for you two? What the hell am I paying you for anyway? You said you could take her. It's three against one."

Wrath continued rambling trash from his mouth while the other two grabbed her, grumbling and cursing at her, one punching her in the eye.

Wrath barked, "No more hits in the face. She's getting married within two hours, and I cannot sell her with bruises all over her."

Married? Who the hell was she marrying?

They dragged her down the passageway and out the back entrance, but she kicked and fought all the way. "So you wish to kill another female, you bastard?"

He ignored her, but she could see on his face that her comment had registered with him. One of the men dragging her asked Wrath, "You've killed before?"

"She's lying."

"The hell I am. I can see it in yer face. It surely takes a big man to push someone down the stairs."

The fury on his face told her exactly how strong his temperament was, but she ignored him, spitting in his face.

They put her on the horse, and he sat her up and said, "You will listen to me, and if you do not, I will pull all of your teeth out with this special tool I took from my son. It's painful, and they'll never grow back, as you know. He'll never want you with no teeth."

Reyna couldn't stop the widening of her eyes, but she recovered as quickly as possible. That was a threat she took seriously.

"You'll keep your mouth closed as we travel through town, or I'll stop and pull one tooth each time you make a sound. A bloody mouth isn't too enticing. Though your lover isn't coming back. I told them Wulf was a traitor."

"He's not a traitor. How could ye treat yer own son that way? Ye are as cruel and evil as he says ye are. Where are you taking me?"

"I owe a baron a wife and since you took my daughter into hiding, I'll take you. He doesn't care which one he has. He needs a cow to give him two sons, then he'll rid himself of you. So shut your vicious mouth, spread your legs and you'll be fine for two years."

"You think I'll marry the baron? Never. Wulf will return for me and he'll see it never happens."

He climbed up behind her, making sure her bound hands were hidden under a mantle he'd grabbed along the way. "Which tooth do you want me to pull first? One word and I'll pull. I have two men to hold you down while I yank."

Reyna closed her mouth as they moved through town. Her mind furiously reviewed all he said. The man had turned his own son in for being a traitor. He also knew that Reyna had freed his daughter from the baron's house.

He continued his rant into her ear as they rode through town. "I knew you went through the secret passageway. It will be boarded up so you cannot escape. And the baron won't care if you have any teeth."

Every time the word tooth came out, she clamped her mouth closed. She couldn't stop herself. It brought images to her mind that couldn't be ignored. But she had to say what was on her mind.

"Ye turned yer own son in? They may hang him."

"I did. And I hope they do hang him. He's a traitor. He deserves it."

"He's no' a traitor."

The man guffawed as they moved out of York, heading toward the baron's castle. "He hasn't told you the truth yet, has he?"

She refused to answer.

"Don't want to talk anymore? Wise decision. Your lover is Scottish. He's never told you, has he? I married his mother, who was a Scottish whore from the Highlands. I tried to beat the

Scottish out of her, but it was nearly impossible."

"So ye killed her by hitting her on the head and shoving her down the stairs?"

Wrath stopped his horse abruptly and yanked her off the horse, motioning to the two other men to stop. "You need to hold her down." He pulled a tool out of his saddlebag and held it up for her to see. "Which tooth?"

Reyna kicked and fought with everything she had. But she also decided it was time to tell Wrath de Gray exactly what she thought of him. "Ye told the English yer son is a traitor? Ye even hope he hangs? What kind of father are ye? Ye are a cruel son of a bitch, ye bloody bastard. Ye sell yer daughter to a cruel bastard. And how much did he pay ye? Do ye sleep well at night knowing how mean ye are? Killed yer own wife, had yer son hanged by the English, and sold yer daughter to a man who kills his wives when he doesn't need them anymore. Ye should be mighty proud of yerself when ye stand in front of the pearly gates. Which way do ye think they'll send ye? Down or up?"

The two men held her on the ground while Wrath came at her with the tool.

She couldn't hold it in any longer.

"Hold her head."

She let out the loudest scream she'd ever uttered in her life.

## CHAPTER SEVENTEEN

THE THREE RODE for at least three hours, though Wulf had no real idea of how long it had been since his mind bounced from one subject to another. Reyna, Tryana, his wicked father, any other Englishman who would recognize him. He knew that he was still in jeopardy of being arrested as long as he remained on English soil.

Once they left the prison, they continued on a common path, but he still didn't dare ask questions. At one point, the man who'd held the key that had opened his prison cell stopped and turned to him. "Maitland Menzie will get ye back to York. I would trust him with my life, so do as he says and Godspeed to both of ye."

Once the one man left so it was just the two of them, he pulled his horse abreast of Maitland's. "Ye have found my sister?"

Maitland nodded. "Reyna marked the site. We made it inside shortly after midnight and she was ready. Though she was already aware of your arrest. But she came willingly and we escorted her to an abbey north of York. I left Cadyn, Ysenda, and Lewis with her."

"And Reyna?"

"Reyna is back at the inn. She's staying inside because I did not want yer sire to find her. He'll be what I call pissing angry once he finds Tryana gone. He'll be looking for someone to take that anger out on, so I thought it best to leave her there. She wished to join me, but I forbid it."

"Mayhap she should have gone to the abbey. She would be safest there."

"She refused. Reyna has her grandparents' blood in her, and of all the offspring, she seems to carry the most stubbornness of her grandparents. She is quick of wit, verra little fear, and highly skilled. Aunt Gwyneth is verra proud of her. Hopes she will help Reyna become a legend in archery to carry on her legacy. I heard she hit a reiver between the eyes while riding her horse. Her grandsire said he'd never seen a shot like that, though he says it was prompted by who the bastard was after, her cousin Isla. They are the best of friends. But where Isla hates battle, Reyna loves the challenge."

They continued on while he absorbed all that Maitland had told him. Reyna was that skilled? She'd proven her skill to him when the reivers had attacked. She'd been punched and kicked and yet still able to use a bow. But he had to admit that leaving her in the same inn his father had chosen worried him. He was a scheming bastard too. If he learned she was there alone, he would do what he could to get his hands on Reyna.

Just to torture Wulf.

"We'll stop at the inn first," Maitland announced when their journey was nearly to an end. "Please keep in mind that if any sheriff sees ye, ye could be arrested and taken back to prison."

"No one knows that better than I do," he said. "I'll not rest until my feet are back on Scottish soil."

"Once we retrieve Reyna from the inn, we'll go to the abbey to retrieve the others, then head straight to Scotland without stopping."

They neared York, entering the town on the second busiest road instead of the one most traveled. Wulf was glad, simply because he still had the feeling that any Englishmen would be watching for him. They'd stripped him of his nice clothing so that he no longer looked like a nobleman, a dirty tunic in place of his doublet, but Maitland had handed him a fresh tunic as soon as they'd left the prison behind.

He'd never thought he'd appreciate a clean piece of clothing the way he had this one.

Nearly to town, they heard three shrieks of a lass not far ahead. Wulf glanced over at Maitland and said, "'Tis Reyna, I'm sure of it."

The loudest scream they'd ever heard ripped through the air. They spurred their horses, Wulf pushing his mount ahead of Maitland's.

Wulf couldn't believe the scene in front of him.

Wrath bellowed, "Who told you that? Who told you I killed my wife? It is all a lie. She fell down the stairs and hit her head."

Wulf jumped off his horse and grabbed his

father by the shoulder, yanking him back, then punching him in the mouth, probably the finest feeling he'd had involving the evil man. "Leave her be. She's going to be my wife."

"The hell she is!" His father took a step back while his other two men grabbed Reyna.

"The numbers are in our favor, Wulf," Maitland announced, not caring who heard him. "Reyna, ye are in our count."

"'Tis my right to kill my father. I watched him kill my mother. Hit her over the head and pushed her down the staircase to her death."

His father paled, glancing nervously at the other men. "You cannot prove such a thing. It was a long time ago and no one will pay you any mind. She's dead and I'm glad of it. Just like I will feel when you are back in prison. You must have escaped, but just like before, I'll call the sheriff again and they'll still hang ye."

"Ye are the one who should be hanged, not Wulf," Reyna shouted before biting the hand on the man to her right and spitting on the one to her left. They both had daggers not far from her throat, but his love didn't seem to care.

"They'll no' hurt ye, love," Wulf said.

"Love," his father sputtered, then spit in the dirt. "What the hell do ye know about love? Ye've never treated me kindly, much less loved me."

"Because ye hated me, ye bloody bastard! I hate ye because ye killed my mother. She was a saint and ye always treated her terribly."

"She deserved it, the Scottish whore."

"I've heard enough," Maitland declared. "Ye have three, Wulf."

"Three?" his father asked when Wulf nodded.

"And two and one, Reyna!" Maitland launched himself at the man on the right of her while Reyna bit the arms of the man on the left.

Her attacker yelped so she spun around and kicked him in the bollocks, sending him to the ground yelping with his hands on his crotch.

Maitland had the other man on the ground with his foot on his chest, squirming until he unsheathed his sword and held it to his throat.

Wulf and Wrath stared at each other, Wrath clearly shocked at the sudden turn of events.

Maitland said, "He's yers, Wulf. Do what ye must but do it quickly so we can be on our way. These two fools were only working for coin. If I let them up, they'll take off running."

The two both nodded, so Maitland let the one up, his sword following him. "If I see ye again, I'll have my blade in the middle of yer belly. Now take yer friend and leave."

Wrath threw various threats and curse words at the two men, but they mounted and disappeared down the lane.

Wulf stood facing his father, his hands on his hips, but then Maitland tossed his sword to him. Wulf caught the hilt and held it in front of his father.

"Why?" he whispered. He had to know. "Why would ye hurt such a beautiful soul? She was a good mother to yer bairns."

The two stared at each other for a long pause.

Finally his sire ground out, "Because you were not my bairns. And the one she did carry of mine died in childbirth. My only son. She probably lost him on purpose. She was a whore and deserved what she got."

Wulf, stunned by this piece of information, took a step back, dropping the sword. Now he remembered. His mother had been carrying not long before she fell to her death. Had she given birth? It all came back to him, the fact that she'd given birth and lost the bairn. And while he expected his sire to feel badly for her, instead he blamed her for it.

Killed her for it.

Reyna called out to him. "He's no' yer sire, Wulf. 'Tis no' worth it to kill him. Dinnae make yerself like him. Ye are nothing like him." Reyna's voice stopped him from doing what he wished to do. "Dinnae give the English another reason to lock ye in a cell."

He glanced over his shoulder, tears misting his gaze, as he stared at Reyna, reaching for her to tug her to his side. "I love ye, Reyna. Forever. My thanks for teaching me what is true and good in the world."

Maitland whispered, "Remember ye are a man accused of treason still in England with a few hours left of light before ye can breathe freely. Reyna is right. Dinnae give them another reason to chase after ye. Ye are safer if ye walk away. They will know who did it if ye do. We had two witnesses."

He nodded, turning to hug Reyna, then lifting

her up onto the extra horse. He'd leave the cruel bastard with no horse and move on with his life. He was nothing like his father. He had no idea who his true sire was, but as long as it wasn't Wrath de Gray, he could move on.

He said to Maitland, "Lead the way. I'll not waste any more time with this worthless bastard."

Reyna whispered, "I love ye too."

Reyna had never been happier. She was no longer a captive, she'd fallen for her captor, and he loved her in return. If they'd just get the hell out of England, she could relax a bit.

They arrived at the abbey, asking for entrance to meet with the abbess.

The woman came out to greet them, Ysenda and Lewis, directly behind her with a brief greeting before they headed to the stables to retrieve their horses.

"Mother Eleonor, I would like to retrieve my sister and take her home with us." Wulf gave her a short bow.

"I'm not sure if she's ready to go home." She looked at Wulf, her gaze quite serious, telling Reyna she was being quite honest. After all she'd been through, the abbey was safer than anywhere else in England. His sire was still searching for a bride for Gareth Ward.

The abbey was not far from the Borderlands, so they would be on Scottish land within an hour. "May I see her, please?" Wulf asked.

It was imperative that they retrieve Tryana and

move quickly, something nuns and abbesses did not do.

"Aye, she said she would meet with you and Reyna for a brief moment."

The abbess waited for the two to dismount before leading them inside the building.

Reyna said to Maitland, "We must return quickly. I know we canno' waste any time."

Wulf took Reyna's hand, a small intimacy that pleased her, so she smiled, and they followed the abbess inside. Once inside the door, she turned to them both and said, "Tryana is deeply traumatized by the events that happened. She does not wish to leave the sanctity of the abbey yet. She fears her father and the baron will come for her. I'll let her explain the rest." She turned around and led them into a small chamber for guests, well-lit with a hearth, a table, and four chairs, and a sideboard with wine and cheese set out already.

Tryana sat in a chair near the hearth. As soon as she saw him, she stood, the fear on her face still evident. "Wulf, ye are hale?"

He moved quickly to greet his sister, giving her a quick hug. "I am, but I must return to Scotland because of the charade I played. I am no longer welcome on English land. Ye will go with me?"

"Where is Papa?" Tryana asked.

The poor lass had bags under her eyes, evidence of how little she'd slept of late.

Reyna understood completely.

"He is still in York. I dinnae believe he will come this way." Wulf leaned over and kissed his sister's forehead. "I was so worried about ye."

"If he is still alive, then I will not leave here yet." She glanced up at her brother, the love in her gaze evident, but so was the fear.

"But why? We will protect ye," Wulf promised.

"How many do you have with you?" Tryana looked from Wulf to Reyna for her answer.

Reyna replied, "Ysenda, Cadyn, Lewis, and Maitland."

Tryana's head shook before she spoke. "Six is not enough. I will remain here until I am certain Father cannot take me back to the baron."

"I dinnae think he will bother ye, Tryana. He admitted to me why he killed Mama and why he hated her. He said he was not our father. That another man is, though he dinnae say who. And ye need no' hide yer Scottish burr anymore. He cannae hurt ye. I will protect ye."

"Wulf, I will remain here until it is safe." She took a step back from him. "Though it pleases me to know he is not our sire, I suspected it. I saw Mama with another man once when you were hunting with Papa. I did not know him, but it does not matter to me. I fear the baron more. I will remain here until I am certain no one will kidnap me away. The baron paid Father a tidy sum of coin for my hand. He will want restitution for my disappearance in some way, and it could be with me."

"Tryana, I must go back to Scotland. They did arrest me for treason, so I must get off English soil. I cannae stay here, or I risk imprisonment."

Cadyn entered from the passageway. "I will stay and protect her."

Reyna and Wulf both spun around to face Cadyn. "Ye will do that, cousin? 'Twould be most wonderful." Reyna said, trying her best to hide her surprise. Cadyn was fierce and loved to follow his grandfather around. Because of that, he was well-trained in sword skills and archery. He'd never allow Wrath near Tryana in the abbey.

"Aye, I will stay. Mayhap Grandpapa will send a larger force, and we can both return together. But I willnae leave her here alone. While the abbey is a safe place against most, one is never sure."

Wulf looked to Reyna. "Would the Ramsay chieftain be willing to send a force back to escort my sister safely onto Scottish land? I could accompany them."

"Aye, Chief Torrian would, and so would my sire."

Tryana leaned over to hug her brother again. "I love you, Wulf, and I will try to speak as we used to again. But I will await a larger force before I leave the sanctity of the abbey."

Wulf said, "Until then, sister."

"Godspeed to all of you, and I thank Cadyn for his protection."

"'Tis my pleasure," Cadyn replied.

Reyna believed him.

# CHAPTER EIGHTEEN

WULF HATED TO leave his sister behind, but she was a grown woman. Her refusal to travel told him much about what she'd been through. There were enough guards at the abbey, and more nearby if the abbess needed them. He had to return to Ramsay land with Reyna and the group. Then he would speak with Logan Ramsay and the chieftain about his situation and traveling back to retrieve his sister.

And hope he could court Reyna. If he had to travel to Black Isle to meet her parents, he would do it.

Once mounted and ready to go, Maitland gathered Ysenda, Lewis, Reyna, and Wulf together.

"Wulf, are ye strong enough to fight yet?"

"Aye, not for long, but I can if I must."

"Reyna, ye now have a full quiver. I am going to trust that Wulf will act honorably escorting ye to Scotland. 'Tis not safe for ye to travel to Berwick with us. I will escort them, then bring a couple of guards with me to return to Ramsay land. I wish to speak with Logan and see if Isla and Grif are ready to return."

They traveled together for about an hour, then the group separated, one headed to Berwick and the other headed for the faster route to Scottish land. As they separated, Maitland said, "Ye have a two-hour trip. Godspeed with ye."

The other group turned toward Berwick and, Reyna called, "Take care of Goldie for me!" She received a wave of acknowledgment from Maitland. She turned to Wulf and said, "I've been worried about my sweet horse but I'm sure they must have found her."

Once they were on their own, Wulf said, "I wish to hear more about your family, but I fear it should wait until we cross the border."

"Aye, we must travel quietly and quickly."

"Do you know exactly where the border is?"

"No' exactly, but I know when we reach the burn we often stopped at, we are well into Scottish land. 'Tis off the main path so we could stop there to sleep. I dinnae like to travel in the dark."

About an hour later, Reyna slowed her horse. "Here. The burn is near here, so we must be on Scottish land. 'Tis through these trees."

"You are certain? My hide depends on it." He grinned at her, and she smiled back.

"Aye," she said as they neared the sound of a babbling brook. "My grandmother loves this clearing. She always made Grandpapa stop here. And I think there is a small waterfall down the path a bit with a cave behind it, her favorite thing. Not a big cave like the Highlands, but a wee one."

She dismounted as close to the waterfall as

possible, then pointed ahead. "There. This is Scottish land, I am certain."

"Wonderful. I wish we had food, but I fear we do not. But we'll find something on the morrow. I promise. I have to admit I am exhausted. I could try to hunt if you like, but I don't know if I could be successful."

"Lucky for ye that I grabbed a hunk of cheese at the abbey. And I saw a bowl of berries on the way out, so I poured some into this sack hidden inside my tunic."

"My, but you are a woman of substance."

"What do ye mean by that?" She tipped her head at him, clearly confused.

"What I mean is that you are always thinking. I can tell you are experienced at being on patrol. You will never starve on Scottish land, I am sure. But I will settle for that this eve if I can hold you for a wee bit before I fall fast asleep on you. I did not sleep a wink in prison last night. I am exhausted."

She moved over and ran her fingers through the tangles in his hair at the side. "I see that ye are tired. I fear I am too. It has been an exhausting trip for both of us."

"Any regrets, lass?" he asked, afraid to hear her answer. He half expected her to stop her horse once on Scottish land and scream at him for kidnapping her.

"Nay. What happened happened. And I love ye, and ye have said ye love me, so I accept the odd way our love has come about." She stepped up on her tiptoes and kissed him on the mouth.

His lips settled on hers, and he deepened the kiss, dueling tongues with her briefly before he pulled back. "Not yet, lass. No more teasing. I need to speak with you before I close my eyes. We must talk."

"I agree. Come, we'll head behind the water. I have a fur on my horse, fortunately, and we can find a dry boulder to sit on. I know it is here."

They settled behind the waterfall, and he said, "Please allow me to explain."

She nodded, taking a bit of cheese and handing a piece to him before he started.

"You know much of my story already. Our upbringing was not the most pleasant because we had a sire who did not love us, just considered us baggage to feed. Though our mother loved us both, making us what we are today, we did not have her for long enough. After she passed, we were made to work for everything. I learned to hunt because of that, so I am decent with my sword and can use a bow, though not nearly as well as you can. Now I understand so much better than I did before." He paused to take a bite of the cheese, sharing the skein of water with her before he continued.

"Once I turned two and twenty, I went out on my own, though I was often prompted by guilt to go back to see my sister. I knew Papa was not kind to her, but he treated her better than me, simply because she was female, I believe. He knew he could gain coin for a betrothal with her because she is a lovely lass. And we have an aunt and uncle, my mother's brother, who watched over us when we were still in the Lowlands. He lived less than an hour away, so he visited often. And Tryana loved to stay with them, Uncle Lowrans and Aunt Cannie."

"Where did ye live? England or Scotland?"

"We lived in the Lowlands of Scotland because my mother was Scottish. But then, after she died, he moved us to a village not far from Berwick, which, as you know, has gone back and forth between the Scots and the English, but is now with the English. I would travel into Berwick, pick up work at the docks, and even did some spying for a short time. That did not work out well for me because I could never leave my sister for long. But I knew it was just a matter of time before my father married Tryana to someone just to get rid of her. I'm sure he waited until he found the coin he wished for her. That is why I had to follow him. I never knew when he would marry her off, so I never left for long."

"So ye considered yerself Scottish? Then how did ye end up with the English army?"

"They offered good pay for someone to lead the garrison at Berwick. I could speak as English or a Scot, so I took the position for the coin. The stories about me were made up."

"What about Emmot? How did ye know him?"

"Emmot was someone I met at Berwick. We worked together, so he went along with me. But we had an understanding that if I was pulled away because of my sire, he would return to Berwick. There was a tavern we frequented, so I knew I could always find him there. And he also understood that if I ever disappeared, it could be for a while. He warned me about deserting the garrison, advising me that I could be arrested for leaving for so long. In fact, he probably returned to make sure he would not get arrested for desertion. He feared it, so I knew if he disappeared, it would be to stay safe. I'll meet up with him again someday. But I wish to hear about your family. If I am to stay truly in love with you, I need to know how many in your family?"

"Hmm... How to answer that honestly. Mayhap hundreds?"

"What?"

"Oh, my wee family is only six, but my beloved clan and Clan Ramsay and Clan Grant and Clan Cameron... mayhap even a thousand ye'll need to meet. Or hear about. The tales go on forever between my grandfather and my great uncle Alex."

"You have ties to Clan Grant? Don't their guards number in the thousands?"

"Aye, they are allies. And adopted cousins. Isla's grandmother, Brenna, is a sister to Alexander Grant, who was famous for battling at Largs."

"But you are adopted cousins? Never mind that now. Can we start with the six? I'll take on ten new ones every sennight."

She giggled and took her last sip of water. "Wulf, ye look too tired to sit up."

"Then may we lie together like we did after I was hurt? I'll keep you close to give you my heat, promise to be honorable, and then you can tell me about the important other five."

"Mayhap, I wish ye not to be honorable," she whispered with a saucy grin.

"Nay, I'll not go to meet yer sire and the Ramsay chieftain after I take your maidenhead. I will act honorably because that is what I promised Maitland. So please do not tempt me. Besides, I truly am so tired I might embarrass myself through no fault of yours, yet you would believe it to be your fault."

"What?"

"Never mind," he said. Standing, he took her hand, not ready to explain a man's worst embarrassment. "Come, we'll sleep on the soft moss rather than the hard stone." He found a spot and settled the two of them, her bottom backed up against him again, and when he did what he feared, she glanced back at him and smiled.

He said, "I'd have to be a priest not to react to your beauty, Reyna. Now ignore it and tell me about the six of you."

Reyna leaned back against him and started. "I have two brothers, both too young to go to battle yet, but one will soon. Hawk is six and ten, while Merek is twelve. My half-brother Tiernay died from the fever when he was eight. And I have a half-sister Kara who is older than me."

He closed his eyes, saying a quick prayer for the Lord keeping Reyna, Tryana, and him safe. And he thanked Him for introducing him to this beautiful woman tucked against him. He didn't know life could be this sweet.

He smiled as she talked about her mother and father, how they'd fallen in love when he had kidnapped her, how he'd love to hear more about that, but he was too tired to speak.

And her best friend was her cousin, who was born on the same night as she was, something else that made him smile.

That was the last he heard.

They arrived on Ramsay land near dusk the next day, greeted by the usual entourage the Ramsays gathered for visitors—Chief Torrian, her dear uncle Gavin, Uncle Cailean MacAdam, and cousin Gregor.

She explained to Wulf as they were approached by the group. "Gavin is Ysenda's sire and rides on the left, and Cailean is father to Ceit and Cadyn. Torrian, the tallest, is chieftain."

"Then you only have six more to introduce me to for this week."

"Well, ye must meet Isla and Grif, though ye have already met them in an odd way. And ye'll be meeting Grandpapa, I am certain, and Aunt Brenna, the healer. Even though she's my great aunt, I still call her auntie."

"Ye are alone, just the two of ye?" Torrian asked once they approached close enough to speak.

Reyna replied, "Aye, Maitland will be along in a couple of hours. He escorted Ysenda and Lewis to Berwick again. He is hoping to come here and bring Isla and Grif back with him."

"And yer escort?" Gavin asked.

"This is Wulfstan de Gray," she said, barely able

to get the words out before Cailean, Gavin, and Gregor unsheathed their swords in unison.

Reyna yelled, "Nay!"

The horses halted, and Uncle Gavin brought his horse up in front of Wulf's horse. "Explain why ye brought an Englishman home with ye, Reyna. One who held my niece hostage in the dungeon."

Reyna glanced over at Wulf, who paled and was still not looking hale. She'd checked his wound this morning when they'd awakened, not pleased to see it was turning to pus. She needed to get him treated. In fact, from where she sat, he appeared feverish.

Wulf held both hands up. "I will not fight any of you. If you allow me entrance, you may bind my hands, and I will explain if you will allow me that chance. I love Reyna, and I was not loyal to the English. My actions were one of a spy. I am a Scot by blood."

The three men sheathed their swords, and Torrian was about to speak when they noticed another horse coming from the castle.

It was her grandsire. He approached the outside of their muddled circle, his eyes on Reyna first, then Wulfstan. Gavin moved his horse back to allow his sire in. While Grandsire's age was clear, his eyes were as astute as ever. Reyna couldn't help but fear what he would do to Wulf once he learned of his true identity. She had to do what she could to prevent it from happening, especially when the man was ill from a wound. "Grandpapa, please allow me to explain."

She feared the worst because he could be a stubborn old man when he wished to be, but this time he surprised her completely, his gaze hard, but no fury as she expected to see. His expression was one of concern but also one of someone who was willing to listen first.

Something unusual for her grandfather.

"Who is it? What has ye all upset, Torrian? I can see it in yer shoulders."

Torrian explained, "Reyna brought Wulfstan de Gray with her. He will allow us to bind his hands until he explains why he is here. I am willing to do that for her if ye are, Uncle Logan."

Reyna bit her lip while she waited for Grandpapa's response, the silence from the rest of the group deafening, which made no sense, but yet it did. No one dared to move a muscle in fear of missing something—a skirmish, a time to guard or go on the offense. It was the Ramsay way. And when Grandpapa struck, most never saw it coming.

The old patriarch gave nothing away with his expression, but said to Torrian, "Allow him in, and I will speak with him first." The rest of the group turned their horses back toward the castle but waited.

Torrian nodded, but then grandfather said, "Reyna, ye are hale enough to ride the rest of the way on yer own? The bruises ye carry dinnae pain ye?"

Gavin and Cailean both swung their heads around to stare at her. Apparently they'd missed the fine shadows of the bruises she still carried from Wrath's men and the ones who tried to attack her when she escaped.

Cailean asked, "They arenae from him, are they?" He pointed to Wulf.

"Nay, Uncle Cailean. They arenae from Wulf. He protected me and was wounded from that encounter. I tried to escape and was attacked in the process. Apparently, some men see me as something to be stolen away."

"And ye fought them off and gained yer own injuries," Grandpapa said. "I'm not surprised that ye would best a few men on yer journey, granddaughter. What about the bruises I cannae see?" he asked, his gaze narrowing as he assessed her.

"I am fine, Grandpapa. Wulf needs tending before I do. He must see Aunt Brenna first. He took a bad wound and is feverish."

"I'm fine, Reyna. I will speak with the man." Wulf nodded to her grandsire. She guessed to give his approval to whatever her grandfather decided.

"Allow him to pass, Torrian. He'll be seen by Brenna first. I'll escort him there while the rest of ye stand down."

She glanced over at Wulf, who was barely able to keep himself on his horse. What he'd gone through at the prison and with his sire had been much more difficult for him than she would have guessed. He was barely able to stay upright. At the present, he appeared overtaken by exhaustion and fever. She wondered what exactly had happened in the prison. She'd probably never know.

She announced just for the sake of it, "And he

gained the wound because of me, so dinnae fault him too much until ye hear all."

Uncle Gavin asked, "All the others are hale?"

"Aye, Ysenda is fine and I just left Cadyn at the abbey. He will be there for a few days. I'll explain later. The others are still at Berwick."

All was quiet as they continued toward the castle, but Reyna could see how unsettled Wulf was and was shocked when Torrian brought his horse up to one side of Wulf and said, "Cailean. The other side."

Reyna said, "Torrian, he willnae hurt anyone."

Torrian turned around to look at her and said, "This is to keep him from hurting himself. He is about to fall off his horse from a fever on our land. Allow me to do my job, Reyna."

Cailean moved inside of her so he was on the other side of Wulf. When they arrived, she dismounted and moved over to help Wulf down, but Torrian pushed her aside. "He's too heavy for ye."

Word traveled fast because they had only passed through half the courtyard when Isla came flying out of the keep and headed straight for Wulf. "Tell me if 'tis true. Is this the bastard who locked Grif and me in the dungeon in Carlisle because it sure looks like him?"

She stopped in front of him and hauled her fist back to strike him, but Torrian stopped her. "He's already sick, Isla. Go until ye hear his story first. Reyna brought him back."

"Reyna!" Isla squealed before launching herself at her cousin, who was now sobbing while she threw her arms around her and hugged her. "I missed ye so much. Ye are hale?"

"Aye, I am fine. But Wulf is Scottish. 'Twas an act to get at his sire. Please dinnae judge him yet. He is feverish from a wound that is my fault."

Isla glanced over as the man walked up the steps to the keep, surrounded by five men.

"I will go with him. Isla, I love him."

Isla scowled. "Ye must be jesting. He kidnapped both of us and ye too."

"Dinnae judge me, cousin. When ye left here, ye hated Grif because he thought ye were inferior. Then ye fell in love with him. Those things happen that we cannae explain." She gave Isla another hug and said, "I must follow him in, but I'm glad ye are here. We shall talk later."

Isla blushed and giggled. "I cannae argue with ye. All that ye said is true." Grif had followed her out, and she leaned in for a hug from him.

"Ye didnae punch him?" Grif asked, watching the group go inside the keep. "I will if ye dinnae."

Isla scowled. "Aye, I promised Reyna I would wait until he was seen by Grandmama."

"Ye have grown, lass," he whispered, kissing her cheek.

Reyna was jealous, but not as much as before. She'd fallen in love, and now she just had to wait to see where it went from there. They had their work to do to get the Ramsay men to believe that it was all a façade, and that he never intended to hurt Reyna or Isla, but she would be diligent until they believed them.

And when they heard the story about his sire, she was confident they would forgive him some of their transgressions.

# CHAPTER NINETEEN

W ULF FELT LIKE a sheep going to slaughter. Isla and Grif had every right to be mad at him since he'd locked them in the dungeon. He had no idea that some of the guards at Carlisle Castle were so cruel. It had been his first time at that castle, so he had not known any of the regular guards there. He had been the one to assign them to the dungeon, but he thought they would be better protected there than running wildly amid all the English he'd seen inside the village walls.

Apparently, he'd made a mistake. He'd heard that Grif had taken a small beating so had stepped in and ordered him to be seen by the man with the worst reputation for inflicting punishment on Scots. But he'd met Steinn along the way and arranged for him to stand in the place of the brute. Steinn had helped Grif get away, but he hadn't known he'd been badly beaten. The job had turned out to be much more involved than he had anticipated when all he'd wanted was coin and a way to get closer to his father in England.

When he'd heard they'd both escaped, he'd

been relieved, especially since he'd pulled guards away from that part of the wall just to make sure they would get away safely.

No one knew of his part in that, even Steinn. At this point, it really didn't matter.

Logan led him into the healing chamber, telling Reyna she'd have to wait until later to talk to the man. She'd gone off with Isla, eager to chatter with her best friend if he were to guess. Before he worried about Reyna, he had to worry about his own safety, hoping no one here would hang him.

Or shoot him in the bollocks. It was her grandmother who had that reputation, wasn't it?

Once he stepped inside the healing chamber, two tall women stood inside, one looking much like the healer and the other looking like the jailer. "Greetings, ladies. I would appreciate any help ye can give me to keep me from losing my leg. I love Reyna with all my heart, and I have transgressions to make up for, and I plan to do so because I love her that much. I am in yer hands. I'm sure ye have heard that I am Wulfstan de Gray, no longer a member of the English garrison but proud to be back on Scottish land."

Logan said, "Fix him, Brenna. I'll explain later, but he's not what everyone thinks. Gwynie knows."

Brenna looked to the woman he assumed was Gwyneth Ramsay, but she said nothing.

Brenna said, "I'll do what I can, Logan. Take yer leave and watch over yer granddaughter and grandniece."

The old warrior left, and the woman said to

him, "I am Brenna Ramsay, grandmother to Isla, the woman you placed in the dungeon, but I am first a healer, so I will fix ye to the best of my abilities. Sit here, please, and tell me all ye have that needs fixing. Everything. And this is Logan's wife, Gwyneth."

"Grandmother to Reyna," Gwyneth added quickly. Her sharp eyes watched his every movement. He didn't doubt she was a fine protector of all her grandchildren and children. "We'll chat after Brenna finishes with ye."

"Agreed," he said, his strength leaving him as soon as he moved toward the spot she'd suggested for him. "I seem to have lost all my strength." His legs trembled, especially the wounded one. The pain increased the longer he stood.

Brenna patted the pallet set on top of a table, a long table, while Gwyneth left. "Call me if ye need me, Brenna."

He sat and began to unwind the bindings around his leg. "I was struck with a sword in two places. Reyna bandaged it for me."

"When?" Her eyes didn't betray any of her feelings.

"Three days ago, I believe. Reyna told me it was a dirty sword. How she can tell, I dinnae know." He knew he was falling back into his Scottish burr, but he didn't care.

"A clean sword would leave a sharper edge to yer wound. One I could stitch easier. Are ye strong enough to handle stitching?"

"Aye. Reyna put an ointment on it after it happened. Do whatever ye must do."

"Ye may thank her later. If she hadnae done that, I would probably be cutting yer leg off. I will clean it, which will hurt, but I believe ye will be able to keep it. I will treat the inside of the wound before I stitch it up."

"Whatever ye need to do. I dinnae wish to lose my leg."

Then the door opened, and Logan came in, handing him a goblet of the breath of life the Scot's were so famous for brewing. "Drink this. 'Tis our finest."

Logan handed it to him, and Wulf swallowed the liquid, enjoying the burn of the golden amber flowing down his throat. He knew it would help to relieve the pain, and he also knew, as any Scot did, it was only given to valued visitors. To refuse it would be an insult to the old warrior and patriarch. "'Tis a fine brew."

Brenna stopped to look at Logan, Gwynie coming in behind him. Brenna gave no inflection to her words but asked, "Why, Logan?"

"Because he did what I asked him to do."

"What?" Brenna's look of surprise didn't escape Wulf, even in his haze of pain and exhaustion.

Gwyneth stood behind her husband and said to Brenna. "Aye. He explained everything to me. Treat him well."

"I look forward to hearing it all." Brenna didn't look up from her work.

"Fix his leg before 'tis too late." Logan poured him another partial goblet.

Wulf drank it down and asked Brenna, "May I close my eyes?"

"Aye, lie down. I hope ye can sleep through this."

He didn't, but the Ramsays made a fine whisky.

---

Reyna looked around the great hall but didn't see Wulf anywhere. He'd disappeared a while ago after Aunt Brenna fixed his leg, but she wished to finish her conversation with her cousin before she followed him. Isla and Grif had left, so she wished to see how Wulf was doing. She thought he'd followed her grandfather to his solar, so she headed down the passageway toward her grandfather's solar.

What were the two discussing?

Almost to the door, she overheard their voices and stopped, frozen by something she thought she heard.

Wulf said, "I dinnae wish for payment. Ye helped save me from that prison, so ye owe me naught. And whatever ye did to get me out, it is much appreciated."

Her grandfather's voice was in a lower tone than usual. "I asked ye to watch over her, and ye did. I promised coin, so I will pay ye."

Watch over her? What the hell was he saying? A cloud descended over her, something she struggled to fight but didn't know how. Words she didn't wish to hear. Words she wished to wipe from her memory, erase from history, tear out of her mind until she never thought of them again.

She feared the truth of them like nothing else. Like a wee bairn, if she could, she would plug her ears just so she didn't hear the truth. Yet she knew she had to know the truth, wouldn't be able to function until she uncovered the meaning behind the words she'd just heard.

Wulf said, "Logan, I've known ye for years. I would have done this as a favor. I know ye promised, but under the circumstances, I'm no' collecting."

"Here is yer coin, and I'll not allow ye to refuse."

Reyna stepped into the doorway, her gaze going from her grandfather to the man she loved. Or the man she thought she loved. "Wulf?"

Her grandsire had a bag of coin on the desk in front of him. "Reyna, leave us, please. This is no' yer concern."

"No' my concern, Grandpapa? I think it is." The look on her dear grandsire's face told her she'd understood everything correctly, the guilt she saw there telling her more than his words. The way he dodged her gaze sticking a dagger in her gut.

Everything she thought she knew in the world just fell out from under her. Everything, if she'd heard right. Or had she misunderstood this bargain between the two men standing in front of her? Two men she thought she trusted and loved more than anything. She could not have heard correctly, though a swirling storm deep in her belly told her she had. She glared at her grandfather. "Ye promised him coin to follow me, to watch over me? Is that what that bag of coin is for—for following me? Is that what this is about?" Reyna was so upset at the implication of what she heard that she thought her head would explode. But she would uncover the truth here and now. Grandfather or not. She loved him, and respected him, but he would not play games with her like that. "Did ye do what I suspect ye did, Grandpapa? Ye ordered a sitter for me as if I were naught more than a bairn?"

Her grandsire said, "Dinnae read into this. Ye are too headstrong for yer own good, Reyna. For God's sake, look at ye. I can see the bruise on your forehead where ye hit a man with yer head. Ye were punched and beaten, ye kidnapped a lass out of a baron's castle, and ye fought off three men without slowing to think about it. What did ye expect me to do? Just let ye go off on yer own without anyone watching over ye?"

"And what of yer other grandbairns? Cadyn, Ceit, Ysenda. What about Isla? She is no' worth it?" Reyna was so upset with the man she wished to slap him. She took more steps toward him but then stopped herself because the closer she came to him, the more she wished to slug him.

"They are not headstrong like ye are, lass. I've known it since ye strode up and kicked a guard in the shin for calling ye ugly when ye were knee high. And when he bellowed, ye picked up a stone and threw it at him. Ye are a powerful force and will be as strong as my Gwynie someday, but no' yet. Ye are too young and inexperienced."

Tears rolled down her cheeks when she strode over to her grandfather and whispered, "What did ye promise him if he pretended to love me? Was that part of the distraction?"

Wulf's face paled, stepping forward. "Reyna, 'tis true what ye overheard, but he didnae ask me to love ye. I fell in love with ye honestly. Dinnae misinterpret this. I dinnae want the coin. Watching over ye was the best thing that ever happened to me." He reached for her, but she held her hand up to him, backing up two steps.

"Dinnae touch me." She thought again of all she'd heard, of how this love of theirs was a façade, of how she couldn't stop her heart from sinking lower than it had ever sunk before.

It broke in two. She now understood the meaning of a broken heart. "Grandsire, how could ye? I hate ye! I will hate ye forever!" Reyna shouted at her grandfather, not caring how he would take it. She would never speak to him again. He was the traitor.

A traitor to her heart. To her soul.

She whirled around and headed out the door, not looking back, not willing to stop for any reason at all. Least of all for Wulfstan de Gray.

The bloody bastard!

She raced to the door and out of the keep, across the cobblestone courtyard, her boots echoing across the inside of the curtain wall. People stopped to see what all the noise was about, but she ignored them.

She searched quickly for a stable boy to saddle a horse for her but finding none she took the closest mount still bridled, her grandsire's horse, and led him out of the stable to the mounting rock and stopped, leaning her head against the big stallion. "Ye will be kind to me, will ye not,

Paz Four? Dinnae throw me. I couldnae handle it." She murmured in his ear, then patted his withers before moving over to the mount, finally climbing on him bareback.

She did not care about anything but being free of anything related to a Ramsay. Settling herself and grabbing the reins at the same time, she bellowed for the guardsmen to open the gate and flew through it, ignoring all the questions thrown at her.

The only thing she paid any attention to was the man who came flying out of the keep directly behind her.

"Reyna, wait! Ye have it all wrong," Wulf bellowed.

And all she could do was yell out the first words in her mind. "Stop trying to speak like a true Scot, ye liar!"

She sent Paz Four into a healthy gallop, something he loved. They flew across the meadow, her hair free and blowing in the wind. She tipped her head back and smiled, the only thing able to make her smile at the moment.

Freedom.

From Wulfstan, his sire, from her grandsire, from the patrol, from everything.

She wished to be alone, vowing to never marry. How could she have thought that her main goal in her life was to marry? Och, aye. That had been when she loved men. How wrong she'd been.

She hated men, so how could she possibly marry? They lied, cheated, turned traitor, and loved to intimidate people just for the power it gave them.

"I dinnae wish for yer power," she mumbled for no one to hear.

The sound of approaching horse hooves came from behind her, so she glanced over her shoulder, not surprised to see Wulfstan on his own stallion, gaining ground. Reyna didn't care what he did. She'd never speak with him again.

No matter how handsome the bastard was.

She was forced to slow down as she approached the forest but entered anyway, taking the path through the woods. Perhaps she'd be set upon by a group of reivers. On this day, she'd offer herself.

She could picture it in her mind. Five randy men surrounding her. "Ye want me? Well ye can have me." She'd rip her clothing off piece by piece. Her scarf, her mantle, her tunic, then her leggings. "Take my maidenhead because I dinnae want it! I'll never use it because no other man will ever touch me again."

Tears blurred her vision at the thought that she'd have easily given the man her maidenhead. The lying bastard, the man arrested by the English for treason, nearly hung by a rope for being a traitor to the English Crown.

He should have been convicted of being a traitor to her heart.

He came up behind her and took her by surprise.

"Get off that horse so we can talk, Reyna. I will follow ye to the end of Scotland and England

and into the sea if I must. Stop and listen! Two minutes."

She had the sudden urge to put a fist in the man's face. Isla had told her how good it had felt when she'd punched the lass who'd lied to send Grif to prison. Perhaps she should stop. Let him know exactly how she felt when they didn't have an audience.

There was a clearing up ahead, so she slowed her horse. "Paz, I'll give ye some refreshment while I listen to the fool behind me." Turning around, she said, "Two minutes is all ye will get."

They stopped in the middle of the clearing, leading both horses to a burn off to one side. Then Reyna ran to the opposite side of the clearing. She definitely feared what she might do if she were close to him.

"Stay away from me, Wulfstan de Gray. And dinnae touch me."

"Fine, just listen to me then. I apologize for what happened. Your grandsire hired me to watch over ye. 'Tis true."

She threw her palm up. "Stop."

"Stop what?"

"Stop talking like a Scot. I knew ye as an Englishman, or have ye forgotten?"

"Nay, I willnae change the way I am. I did what I had to do to protect ye. I had someone arrange for me to come in as the dreaded, cruel English captain. It was all false. I had Emmot go around and spread rumors about me so the others would fear me. I did that before I was hired to protect ye just to gain access to my sire who is English. But the rest was because I needed some things to take place so I could protect ye."

"And did my grandsire ask ye to pretend like ye were in love with me just so I would obey ye? Were all those kisses false too?"

"Nay, I kissed ye because I wished to kiss ye. I wouldnae kiss a woman for any man, not even your grandfather."

"Well, ye can have them all back! It will never happen again, ye lying bastard."

"I lied to the English, not to ye."

"Ye did no' lie to me? Then I knew when ye kidnapped me that I need no' fear for my life when ye pulled me away from Berwick? Did ye even stop to consider that once we headed to York that I feared death because no one from my patrol knew where I was? Why did ye no' tell me all from the start? Or what about the time yer sire was about to pull my teeth out with your tool?"

"My sire is a liar. 'Twas no' my tool, and I've never pulled anyone's teeth out. I couldnae tell ye from the start because I had to keep the façade going or I'd be hanged by the English, Reyna. Can ye no' see that?"

"How did that work out for ye? Seems they wished to hang ye without my help."

He planted both palms into his face as if he'd never get her to understand. He was right about that. Her grandfather hired him to protect her, so he kidnapped her, told her he was a leader in the English garrison, and dragged her to York without any explanation.

"So ye just stole me away, made me think I was

captive. Did ye hire all those men to stare at me too? Just to make me think I needed ye as my protector?'

"Nay, are ye daft, lass? Ye are beautiful. They wanted ye for real and 'twas no' always pleasing to protect ye. Have ye no' thought of that? Do ye think I enjoyed having to fight to protect ye? Sleeping on the floor in front of the door in that inn because so many men wished to buy ye? Taking the wound in my leg when ye ran away? What the hell, Reyna? Ye were a nightmare to protect."

That did it. He would not get away with insulting her.

She took off running straight at him and shoved him as hard as she could. "A nightmare? A nightmare, ye say? Did I *ask* ye to protect me? Nay. Ye should have left me alone. I hate ye! How do ye think I felt when I believed I was abducted by the cruelest man in all of England? That ye might kill me at any given moment? Or ravish me?"

He caught himself, standing strong against her shove. And that made her angrier. She punched his arm, and swung at him, slapping his chest over and over again. "Hit me. Go ahead, the cruelest man in all of England. Hit me, slap me. Do whatever ye wish to me."

She pushed against him, slapped him, and punched his arm. "Come, scary Wulf. Hit me. Ye are a cruel man. Hit me, punch me, make me shut my mouth."

"Nay, I willnae." He stood there, his arms held

out from his sides, allowing her to hit him over and over again, but she didn't understand why. "I will never hit ye, Reyna. I love ye truly, and I'll no' deny it."

"Why no'? I'm just a foolish lass, someone whose emotions ye can play with. Did ye know that before I met ye, I loved men? Now I hate them. I hate them! I hate ye!"

Then she did the thing she'd been aching to do since she learned of his betrayal.

Reyna hauled her fist back and punched him directly in his jaw.

# CHAPTER TWENTY

HELL, BUT HE'D deserved that. Reyna caught him good just below his jaw, and he didn't blame her. How could he? How ironic the way this had all played out.

Before he'd met Reyna, he'd hated everyone but his sister. Curse it all, but he'd tried to convince Tryana to go with him anywhere but where their father lived. First into the Highlands, then into Berwick, but the farthest he could get her to travel was to their uncle's home. She'd refused all his suggestions, fearful that their father would kill them the same way he did their mother.

Apparently, Tryana had been correct to respect that fear.

But if not for his dear sister, he'd have left long ago. He hated his life. Wished to be allowed to live alone, not be bothered by anyone, but he'd made the mistake of needing the coin. That blasted coin that betrayed him. How could he make Reyna understand that following her was the best thing that ever happened to him? If not for her, he'd become a recluse. But now he wished to marry her, cherish her, join her clan, raise their bairns together. He adored Reyna. And her clan. Every last one of them he admired. What the hell had she done to him?

And as she'd just said, because of him she now hated all men.

Especially him.

Who else was so powerful within that they could change him from hating people and living as a recluse to wanting to, nay, looking forward to, meeting hundreds of her relatives?

She swung at him again, and he let her, his gaze locking on hers. How could he make her understand what she meant to him?

Everything.

"Reyna Matheson, I love ye, so I willnae ever strike ye. Never!" Her hands continued to swing at him, though she was losing her strength, an odd catch in her throat. "I promise to spend my life loving ye and praying that someday ye'll return my love. A chance. Please give me a chance. Give our love a chance to survive and flourish. There will never be anyone for me but ye, Reyna Matheson. There is no other woman like ye—strong, beautiful, loving. None."

The tears started. "Hit me. Please hit me back, Wulf. Show me how ye truly feel. Ye had me. Ye could have tortured me. I thought I hated ye, I feared ye, then ye made me fall in love with a false person, one who was created for my grandsire. How could ye hurt me so? I loved ye, and ye plunged a dagger into my heart. This was all for my grandsire, not me."

She was losing her spirit, her force, her strength.

"Nay, ye'll no' lose that spirit I love so, Reyna. 'Tis one of the reasons I fell in love with ye. Ye have such a powerful spirit, a strong core that ye've spent years building, learning from the women in yer clan. Ye are a force unlike any other. Hit me harder. I deserve it. But ye must believe me when I say that I had no intention of falling in love with ye."

"Aye," she whispered as the tears flowed freely down her cheeks. "'Twas all a plan. A big plan created by ye and my grandsire. How can I ever love again?" Her hands landed on him, but she couldn't even look at him anymore. The pain was too much for her broken heart. He could see it all in her gaze.

Bloody hell, he'd not lose this woman he adored more than life. "Reyna, please, believe me." He dropped to his knees in front of her. If that's what it would take to show her how much he loved her, then he would do it. He'd beg, ignoring the pain in his leg.

"Please believe me. I love ye, Reyna. Ye are my world. I wish to love ye, to hold ye, caress ye. I wish to make ye my wife, make ye mine forever, have bairns together. Sit by the hearth when we are old together."

"Nay, 'tis all a lie. A great big lie." Her tears broke into sobs. Deep, heart-wrenching sobs. Still on his knees, he reached up and cocooned her hands with his. "I beg ye to forgive me, to believe me. But ultimately, I wish to make ye happy. So if, after all I've said, if ye wish for me to walk away, I will, but know ye will have ripped out my heart and stomped on it. I love ye now more than ever. I fell in love with ye, but 'twas never planned. Yer grandsire never said a word about loving ye or pursuing ye."

Her sobs continued, and she closed her eyes, wailing from her heart.

"My only plan was to search for my sire, find the bastard to kill him. I wished to save my sister from a horrific marriage. Yer grandsire found me when I was on my way. He offered me coin, and I needed it. Aye, 'tis true that I had nae feelings for ye at all when I started. In fact, I considered ye a spoiled noble lass. But ye changed it all. Even my heart." A tear welled up in the corner of his eye, something he'd not done in years.

"I never knew what love was until I met ye, Reyna."

There. Wulfstan said it. He loved Reyna, adored her, and didn't want to live without her.

Her breathing hitched, and she opened her eyes, swiping at the tears all over her face.

"Tell me what to do, Reyna. Love ye or leave ye. 'Tis yer choice."

She let out a keening wail and fell against him, wrapping her arms around his shoulders. "I love ye, Wulf. Please love me, never leave me. I couldnae handle losing ye again."

He let out a sigh, cupping her face with his hands. "Lass, ye never lost me. I never stopped loving ye."

"But I thought ye did. Or I never thought ye did. Or…"

"Never ye mind." He kissed her hard on the

lips, and she returned it, deepening the kiss as their lips melded together in a hot mating ritual that left him breathless. His tongue mated with hers, and he ravaged her, and she met all of his moves with her own. Groaning, he lowered her to the soft mossy ground beneath them, settling himself on top of her.

"Say aye, Reyna. Tell me ye will marry me, be my wife forever. Please."

"Aye, aye, aye! I love ye, Wulf. Love me, please. I canno' wait any longer."

"Are ye sure, lass? We cannae go back from this. Marry me on the morrow?"

"Nay, we can handfast, then plan a wedding when everyone is back. I dinnae wish to wait to be together. We can handfast and marry when all can celebrate with us."

That would suit him fine. He would want Tryana here too.

"I pledge my troth to ye, Reyna Ramsay Matheson, and we shall live together as husband and wife from this day forward." He took her hand in his and intertwined their fingers. "But I would feel better about this if ye would stop yer tears." He kissed one tear from her cheek.

"If I cry now, they are happy tears. I pledge my troth to ye, Wulfstan de Gray, forever ye shall be mine."

He couldn't stop the low growl from coming out of his chest, so he kissed her again, this time with a passion he never thought he would have, his need for this woman more than he understood.

His tongue stroked hers and they explored each other until they were both breathless.

~~~~

Reyna was so in love with this man that she didn't know how to control her need for him, didn't know what to do next, so she decided to follow his lead. He ended the kiss, his lips grazing across her forehead, then to her jawline, then her neck.

"I wish to feel all of ye against me."

She had already begun to remove her trews and tunic, slipping out of her leggings with ease, but then she tugged on his tunic. "Yer leg, Wulf."

"Dinnae worry about my leg, Reyna. 'Tis most fine and I dinnae feel any pain when I am with ye. I am well bandaged."

His lips settled on hers again and before she knew it, he had removed all of his clothing and half of hers. All that she had left was a short chemise. Behind its thin fabric, her nipples tingled and tightened at the coolness of the air.

"Here," he said, rolling her onto her side so he could slip his tunic underneath her. "The ground is cool." He kissed one side of her buttock, something that embarrassed her all the way to her toes.

He settled her back down, then lay beside her before his mouth settled on the center of her belly, then trailing up to her breasts. He took one nipple into his mouth, suckling her through the fabric of her chemise while his hand teased her other nipple until it peaked. "Ye are a beauty, Reyna."

His lips traveled from one spot of her body to another, a moan escaping her lips when he found her other nipple. She cried out, her hand grabbing a fistful of his hair while he tortured her with his mouth and hands, her voice reacting with whimpers and her body arching in ways she couldn't control. Her hands traveled to his chest, to his nipples, then down until she grasped onto him. He moaned and stilled her hand. "Ye cannae or I'll spill my seed like a laddie. Ye arenae ready yet."

"But I want to touch ye," she whimpered.

"Not yet," he said before his lips descended on hers again and his tongue probed hers, a delicious assault that she tried to return.

His fingers brushed over her breasts while they traveled lower and she strained against the fabric in her chemise, wishing it wasn't there. Somehow he tugged it off without slowing their love dance one bit and she cried out when his mouth settled on her nipple again, his teeth scraping the tender point while his hand traced a line down across her belly and below, finding the tangled curls at the apex of her thighs. Gently he slipped his fingers through her folds, seeking her entrance. She gasped at the surprising intrusion and he lifted his lips from hers to look into her eyes. "Lass, you understand what we are about to do? We can stop now if you want to wait. I can pleasure you with my mouth and hands but not breech your maidenhead."

Reyna's body seemed to answer for her as she strained against his hand in a silent plea for more. "Oh, Wulf, nay, I dinnae want to stop or wait. I was just surprised… I'll try no' to gasp again."

"Oh, no, lass, your soft sounds feel like kisses and strokes. The sound of your desire makes my own desires burn hotter." He lowered his lips to hers and she groaned into his mouth again. He moved his fingers through her curls and folds as she moved against him, seeking more until he found the pearl of her pleasure at the top of her sex.

Shy at first, she fought the urge to open herself to him until he touched that spot on her core that was like releasing the spring on a lock, her thighs spreading for him as her need grew. His finger pulsed inside her in a pattern she needed, rocking against him to bring him in deeper. He continued to tease her sensitive flesh as he murmured sweet loving words against her ear, urging her to enjoy the feel of his fingers as he stroked her core and pressed against the center of her pleasure. He licked her nipples and scraped them gently with his teeth, and a tension built inside her that she did not understand.

"Please, Wulf." She felt wicked and shameless but did not care, instead arching her back against him, unsure of what she needed, but convinced he could sate her need.

He gently removed his fingers from her and positioned himself where his hand had been, She felt their bodies meld together and he whispered in her ear, "Forgive me for hurting ye," as he moved against her entrance, the heat of his hard member filling a need she didn't know she had until he probed deeper, thrusting in and out in a pattern she wished to be stronger, more direct... More.

With one hard thrust, he broke through her barrier and stopped, the pinch of pain freezing her.

"Tell me when," he whispered.

She fought the tears and the wish to push him out because she knew she would need to finish this. Now was not the time to run away from a little pain. "Go ahead," she whispered, fearing the worst, but surprised to feel the need blossoming inside her again until she reached a feverish pitch. "More," she said. "Harder."

He stretched her insides, the warm throb of him, the closeness of their flesh fueling a need inside her, a sense of wonder at this new experience. Her fingers found the corded muscles of his back, digging into him to push more, harder, faster. Whatever it took.

Something inside of her exploded with pleasure, and she screamed his name as her body shuddered violently in his hands, and he answered with a shout and a deep thrust that nearly touched her core as his seed shot into her.

A sudden sense of wonder and joy suffused her body, of attaining what she'd always been seeking, of newfound knowledge of what life was meant to be.

Exactly what she'd always known deep inside

her. She had wanted a man in her life for a long time, and now she understood why.

Wulf kissed her chin, and her mouth, then her cheek. "Did I please ye, my lady?"

She giggled, the sound coming out oddly between the pants she couldn't quite stop, nor did she wish to. The experience was too exhilarating to rush. Their flesh molded as if it were one, every part of them, sweat mingling together as they regained their senses. She ran her fingers up the muscles in his upper arm, reveling in the hardness there. "Aye, ye did, and ye know it. And ye?"

"Better than I would have ever thought possible."

"So ye will stay handfasted with me?"

"Aye, forever. Ye'll no' back out on me now so dinnae even think on it."

She stopped and cupped his face. "Never. Ye are exactly what I've needed in my life, Wulf. I love ye with all my heart."

"And ye just made me the happiest man possible. Something I thought was impossible."

# CHAPTER TWENTY-ONE

WULF HELPED REYNA clean up, finding a water skein on one of the horses before they returned to the castle.

"Think ye anyone will know?" she asked.

"I think someone might suspect. But we are handfasted, and I stand by my word. Ye are my wife now." He wouldn't look at it any other way.

They made their way back to the great hall, and Reyna leaned over to whisper in his ear, "I'm glad Grandpapa is no' here. I'm no' ready to forgive him yet."

"Reyna, he did it because he loves ye, and no other reason. Someday we shall have a daughter of our own and I may do the same thing. 'Tis not easy for a lass in this world of ours. But I think ye understand it better now."

"Ye are correct. But I'll still no' look for him yet."

"I wouldn't wait too long to speak with him and forgive him. Time is too precious to let it go. I wish I'd told my mother how much I loved her, but I hadn't told her in a long time."

"She knew by yer actions, I'm sure, Wulf."

"I hope that is true." He glanced around the hall and said, "I need to speak with Isla and Grif."

They found the two in a deep discussion with Torrian, so they asked if they could join them. He held the chair for Reyna, who took the seat next to Isla, giving her best friend a swift hug before sitting.

"I'm here to make amends, if possible. I'll tell ye what I think ye need to know and Reyna can answer any other questions."

"Agreed," Torrian said. "And I'll stay."

Wulf decided to start right in with his explanation. He would do anything to be accepted in this clan. "I was born to an English father and a Scottish mother. We lived in the Lowlands, until I watched my father push my mother down a staircase after hitting her in the head with an iron doorstop. I was informed he was traveling to England so I thought if I took on the role of a captain in the English garrison, one not assigned to a major battle, that I could keep an eye on my father, make sure he did not wed my sister to someone unacceptable to me."

"So ye joined as a spy?" Torrian asked.

"Basically, aye. I was never loyal to England in my heart. Ever since my mother died, I've considered myself only Scottish."

Reyna squeezed his hand. "And ye found out ye are probably all Scottish."

"Aye, when I finally managed to get my sister away from my sire, he told me why he hated us so. We were not of his blood. Tryana was aware of the possibility, but I never was."

Wulf went on to explain his part when they were at Carlisle Castle, that he'd known nothing of the beating that Grif had experienced or he would have had someone pay for it.

Isla said, "But yer reputation. How did ye gain such a horrible one so quickly?"

"All false. I had a friend spread the rumors and it worked. And I met Steinn and he told me of his brother, so I switched him out so he could help ye escape."

"Ye helped my brother?" Grif's shocked expression told all.

"I did."

"Do ye know where my brother is now? We left so quickly that I know no' what happened to him."

Reyna explained, "He was with Dyna's group at Berwick Castle. He said he's going to stay with ye, Grif. He said he'll join either clan, whatever ye wish to do—Ramsay or Matheson."

Wulf said, "I'm going to add one more thing. I love Reyna with all my heart and I consider her to be my wife. Whenever she tells me the time is nigh, we will marry. I will do whatever it takes to be accepted by Clan Ramsay and Clan Matheson."

Torrian stood and said, "If Reyna accepts ye as her husband, then we will accept ye. Though I never answer for my uncle, Logan. I know there was something unusual happening there, but he'll tell me when he is ready. I trust his judgment."

Isla gave a little squeal once Torrian walked away. "Ye know what this means, do ye no'?"

Reyna gave her cousin a puzzled look. "No' exactly."

"We can get married together after the mission is over! Grif willnae care, will ye?"

"Whatever makes ye happy. And that we wait for Steinn."

Reyna squealed and hugged her cousin. "What a great idea! I canno' wait!"

***

Reyna glanced down at her husband. Wulf was sound asleep, still healing from his wound and the hell he'd lived through, so she decided to leave him be. She'd promised to sleep with Isla this night like old times, but she had the distinct need to be alone for a bit.

Away from everyone, a chance to think about all that had happened because it had all happened so quickly. What better place than on the top of Ramsay Castle so she made her way down the passageway and opened the heavy stone door that led to the staircase. Reyna climbed the drafty stairs, pushed open the door, then leaned on the cold stone of the parapets, beginning to understand how her great uncle Alex had said it was the best place in the world. A place to be alone, think on everything without interruption.

Uncle Alex had said the beauty of Scotland could fix anything. The wind whistling through the trees, the scamper of the squirrels, the smell of the pines. The feeling of being that much closer to heaven. And the feeling of loving and knowing you are loved in return. Loving Wulf had changed her more than she would have ever guessed. She had a sense of happiness that she'd never had, giving her an understanding of Isla and Grif and their whirlwind love.

Hers had been full of a wee bit more turmoil, but all was well. She loved Wulf, and he loved her. Scotland and the parapets were the best place to be.

Uncle Alex was right about that.

The door opened, and a woman peeked her head around the corner. "May I join ye, lass?"

"Aye, Grandmama. Ye know I adore ye, and every time I am with ye is special. Did the stairs no' bother ye?"

"Aye, a wee bit, but I made it on my own," she said rubbing her knee first, then her hip. The woman known as Gwyneth Ramsay to the world, the best archer in all the land, came out and hugged her, then leaned against the stone with her, staring out over Ramsay land. "Ye know I love yer grandfather with all my heart."

Reyna nodded. "I know. And I still love him too."

"No one knows him better than I do. So I feel I'm the best judge to let ye know something important."

"What?" She had no idea where her beautiful grandmother was going with this, her long gray hair waving in the wind, her body still thin but muscular because she never rested even though her bones pained her at times.

"Logan can be a real pain in the arse."

Reyna spluttered, if she'd have had a drink,

she surely would have spit. "Grandmama!" She'd never expected that.

"When I met him, Logan Ramsay was stubborn, belligerent, and often times a fool. But I fell in love with him. Not because of his looks or his wit, but at first because of how he loved Torrian and Lily. With a ferocity that frightened me. The way he loved Ashlyn and Gracie, the way he took care of the wee ones, watching out for those who couldn't protect themselves.

"When I figured out that he loves everyone with that same kind of ferocity, I decided I wished to be one of those people. I wanted him to love me like that, and he has."

"Oh, Grandmama, he adores ye. Everyone knows that." She reached for the few hairs blowing in her eyes and smoothed them back, now able to see the tears in her grandmother's eyes.

She sniffled, gripping Reyna's hand. "I know. He can hate with the same ferocity. There is no partway with Logan Ramsay. But sometimes, that powerful love gets in the way of his ability to think clearly. He has an uncanny way of knowing exactly what bairns need, better than adults. He has always been a wonderful father and a grandfather too. But he sees things in young ones that I don't. Things I don't comprehend. He gets into their minds, looks at them as individuals before any other adult does."

Reyna knew where this was going. She hadn't spoken to her grandsire since that fateful time in his solar. She and Wulf made up, but her grandfather had been the cause of it all, and she hadn't forgiven him yet. She'd hoped the parapets could give her clarity on the situation.

"And he knows exactly what makes each one of ye special. I trust him completely there. He has an extra sense."

"Ye know I love Grandpapa, but I am still mad at him."

"And he will always love ye as I do. Will ye listen to him?"

She didn't think she was ready, but perhaps up here on the parapets, away from all the prying ears and eyes, was the right place. She nodded, and her grandmother hugged her and stepped back. "Grandmama, by the way, ye and Mama gave me the strength to carry on in all the situations I found myself in. Thanks to ye both and yer teachings, I was able to keep my head and help myself at every step. I thank ye for that. I love you for it!"

"Ye are a strong lass, and I am forever proud of ye, Reyna." She turned and opened the door for her grandfather.

"Logan, be kind and be honest." She scowled at her husband, something that made Reyna smile.

"Aye, Gwynie. I know when I'm wrong, and ye need no' remind me."

Reyna watched the looks pass back and forth between her grandparents, something she loved to watch. What an inspiration they were to her. To all her cousins.

"I'll leave ye two alone," Grandmama said,

closing the door then going down the stairs, her boot heels clicking on the stone steps.

"Granddaughter," he said, nodding, and looking very uncomfortable. There was a time he was known as the Beast of the Highlands, though he didn't look beastly at the moment.

"Grandsire," she whispered, waiting to see what he had to say.

"Ye know I'm no' good with words."

"But ye are usually good with feelings, Grandpapa. How did ye get it so wrong this time?" She could not understand what had possibly possessed him to do what he did.

"I stand by my actions. I'll beg yer pardon for upsetting ye, but I had nae idea ye would fall for the brute, did I?"

"But I feared for my life with him. I…"

He held his hand up to stop her, so she ended her tirade, if a bit too early. She would always love and respect him, the many fond memories of their wonderful times together firmly locked in her heart.

"Reyna, I didnae do the same with the others because ye are different. Ye…" He choked on his last word and stared out over the landscape, taking a long pause. "Ye think ye are the same as yer cousins, but ye arenae. Did any of yer female cousins wrestle all the lads to the ground whenever they got mad at them? Did they ever fist fight five male cousins at once? Or try to wrestle a wild boar on their own, for God's sake? I could almost see that boar's tusk going right through yer belly. Thank the Lord that Molly could shoot so well."

"I know all of that, but the kind who needs more protection than the others? Because I'm a terrible archer? I cry too much? Why, Grandpapa? Why would ye insult me so?"

"Ye dinnae understand." He gave her that Ramsay glare used to intimidate, but she would not concede because she wished to know the truth. "I love ye the same as the others, but..."

"Help me, please. I wish to understand."

"Because ye are... What ye are becoming is..."

She waited, just now understanding how difficult this was for him, this admission or whatever it was to be. He fumbled for his words, tugged on his gray beard, and sweat broke out across his brow in the wind. But then he brought his eyes to hers. "I thought it would be Sorcha, but her heart is too big, something I do indeed admire. I thought mayhap Maggie or Molly, but they had some horrible memories from their childhood that kept them meek at times. And Brigid was so loving and warm, and she never had the interest in archery that ye have. She learned it well, but she didnae have that spark, that extra dexterity she needed. 'Tis a special mix of intelligence, guts, and talent. 'Tis..."

He stumbled again, pausing with his thoughts, so she waited.

"Reyna, I dinnae know how else to say it, but ye are exactly like my Gwynie. Strong, foolish, headstrong, smart, and so skilled. No one else can stand head-to-head with a man and beat them at whatever ye choose. Hellfire, but ye butted a man in the head with yer own head. Ye are out of yer mind sometimes, just like Gwynie. I've always had to protect her, guide her, and now I must protect ye in the same way. Ye could carry her reputation on, if ye wish it. No one else has the abilities ye have. Ye are the Gwynie of the next generation. Ye have the strength of mind that goes with the skills of yer grandmother. And because of it, ye'll get yerself into more trouble too. But I hope ye'll find it in yer heart to forgive this old man."

"Oh, Grandpapa. I forgive ye. Ye know I love ye." She burst into tears and hugged him, knowing she'd never share this moment with anyone.

But it would stay in her heart forever.

# EPILOGUE

WULF SCRATCHED HIS chin as he sat on his horse, watching Reyna demonstrate all her skills as a horsewoman. He didn't blame her for loving to ride, especially up here in the lands where the wind blew so sweet, the trees boasted a color green unlike anywhere else. And the mountains in the distance were unlike any he'd seen before.

His sweet wife could ride better than anyone he knew. It had been a sennight since they left the abbey, and his leg was nearly back to normal thanks to the skills of Brenna Ramsay. Yet he was unsettled in his sleep every night.

Torrian had sent a force to get Tryana and Cadyn back, including his sire, Cailean, but they had not returned. They should have returned last eve, but they did not.

No messenger had been sent by the abbess or Maitland. Something had happened.

But what?

Had the baron or his father breached the abbey? Had they stolen her away? Was Tryana missing already?

Reyna stopped her horse next to him, breathless from the exertion but smiling with joy. She leaned over and kissed him. "Ye are thinking too hard, my love. My parents are on their way. They should be here before nightfall tomorrow. Are ye afraid to ask for my hand?"

"Nay, 'tis no' the problem at all. I look forward to meeting the two people who brought ye into the world and raised ye to have such a big heart and a strong core."

"What is it then?" She peered at him, but he didn't know exactly how to explain it to her.

A horse appeared across the meadow, flying directly toward them. One who was just arriving on Ramsay land, two other horses now joining the lead horse.

Reyna frowned. "Oh, I dinnae like this."

"Who is it?"

"Dyna. The other leader of the patrol. If she's coming it means something has happened. Ceit and Alaric are behind her."

"I knew it."

"What?" Reyna asked.

His gut dropped because he knew what Dyna would say. Something had happened, and it had to do with Tryana.

He should have killed his father when he had the chance.

Dyna approached, stopping her horse directly in front of them, her breathing slowing so she could catch her breath. Ceit and Alaric stopped behind her.

"'Tis Tryana." He stated what he knew the truth was, without a doubt.

Dyna nodded. "I had a dream about her, so we traveled to the abbey the next morn."

"And?" he asked impatiently, his heart thudding in his chest.

"Tryana and Cadyn are both gone. They left in the middle of the night. Some of Torrian's patrol is out searching for them."

Wulf moved his horse to leave, but Reyna stopped him. "Wait. Dyna is a seer. See what she has to say. Never leave without all the information ye can gain."

He turned around and said, "Fine. Know ye anything else?"

Reyna added, "Did ye see them in yer dream, Dyna?"

"We know naught for sure, but in my dream, I did see them together."

"Where were they?" Wulf persisted.

"They're being chased by two monsters. I'm sorry, but 'twas all I could see. I've tried to see more, but it doesnae change."

Reyna paled and gripped his hand. "Yer father and the baron."

Wulf feared she was right. Reyna's parents would have to wait. "Love, we're going to the Borderlands."

### THE END

www.keiramontclair.com

DEAR READER,
Thanks for continuing on this journey with me. Clan Ramsay, Highland Hunters, and the rest will continue in Cadyn and Tryana's story, coming next to you.

Happy reading!

*Keira Montclair*
www.keiramontclair.com

# NOVELS BY KEIRA MONTCLAIR

## **HIGHLAND HUNTERS**
THE SCOT'S CONFLICT
THE SCOT'S TRAITOR

## **HIGHLAND HEALERS**
THE CURSE OF BLACK ISLE
THE WITCH OF BLACK ISLE
THE SCOURGE OF BLACK ISLE
THE GHOSTS OF BLACK ISLE
THE GIFT OF BLACK ISLE

## **THE CLAN GRANT SERIES**
#1- RESCUED BY A HIGHLANDER-
Alex and Maddie
#2- HEALING A HIGHLANDER'S HEART-
Brenna and Quade
#3- LOVE LETTERS FROM LARGS-
Brodie and Celestina
#4-JOURNEY TO THE HIGHLANDS-
Robbie and Caralyn
#5-HIGHLAND SPARKS-
Logan and Gwyneth
#6-MY DESPERATE HIGHLANDER-
Micheil and Diana
#7-THE BRIGHTEST STAR IN THE
HIGHLANDS-
Jennie and Aedan

#8- HIGHLAND HARMONY-
Avelina and Drew
#9-YULETIDE ANGELS

## THE HIGHLAND CLAN
LOKI-Book One
TORRIAN-Book Two
LILY-Book Three
JAKE-Book Four
ASHLYN-Book Five
MOLLY-Book Six
JAMIE AND GRACIE-Book Seven
SORCHA-Book Eight
KYLA-Book Nine
BETHIA-Book Ten
LOKI'S CHRISTMAS STORY-Book Eleven
ELIZABETH-Book Twelve

## THE BAND OF COUSINS
HIGHLAND VENGEANCE
HIGHLAND ABDUCTION
HIGHLAND RETRIBUTION
HIGHLAND LIES
HIGHLAND FORTITUDE
HIGHLAND RESILIENCE
HIGHLAND DEVOTION
HIGHLAND BRAWN
HIGHLAND YULETIDE MAGIC

## HIGHLAND SWORDS
THE SCOT'S BETRAYAL
THE SCOT'S SPY
THE SCOT'S PURSUIT

THE SCOT'S QUEST
THE SCOT'S DECEPTION
THE SCOT'S ANGEL


## THE SOULMATE CHRONICLES TRILOGY
#1 TRUSTING A HIGHLANDER
#2 TRUSTING A SCOT
#3 TRUSTING A CHIEFTAIN

## STAND-ALONE BOOKS
ESCAPE TO THE HIGHLANDS
THE BANISHED HIGHLANDER
REFORMING THE DUKE-REGENCY
WOLF AND THE WILD SCOTS
FALLING FOR THE CHIEFTAIN-
3$^{RD}$ in a collaborative trilogy
HIGHLAND SECRETS -
3$^{rd}$ in a collaborative trilogy

## THE SUMMERHILL SERIES-
## CONTEMPORARY ROMANCE
#1-ONE SUMMERHILL DAY
#2-A FRESH START FOR TWO
#3-THREE REASONS TO LOVE

# ABOUT THE AUTHOR

Keira Montclair is the pen name of an author who lives in South Carolina with her husband. She loves to write fast-paced, emotional romance, especially with children as secondary characters.

When she's not writing, she loves to spend time with her grandchildren. She's worked as a high school math teacher, a registered nurse, and an office manager. She loves ballet, mathematics, puzzles, learning anything new, and creating new characters for her readers to fall in love with.

She writes historical romantic suspense. Her best-selling series is a family saga that follows two medieval Scottish clans through four generations and now numbers over thirty books.

Contact her through her website:
www.keiramontclair.com

# ABOUT THE AUTHOR

Made in the USA
Monee, IL
03 October 2023

43892510R10129